The Concrete Jungle

Phil Morgan II

PublishAmerica
Baltimore

ISBN: 1-4241-4156-7
PUBLISHED BY PUBLISHAMERICA, LLLP
www.publishamerica.com
Baltimore

Printed in the United States of America

For my grandfather,
who never got to read this,
and my wife,
who had to read it too much.

For reasons too complex to express I find myself indebted to several people:

To Melvin Johnson, for numerous and tedious brainstorming and editing sessions.
To my family, for support even when it was unwarranted.
To Publish America, for taking a chance on my work.
To Jerry Thompson, for his diligent work hammering a vocabulary into my head.
To my friends, for putting up with me shoving manuscripts into their hands.

The Concrete Jungle

Phil Morgan II

The Concrete Jungle

"That's life in the Concrete Jungle."
—The Crimson Avenger, epitaph

The moon rose like an angry god over the concrete jungle. Spilling sickly light onto the detritus of civilization and illuminating the dark heart of humanity with its ascent, the nightly visitor impassively observed as it made its rounds. Tonight the moon would be busy with its appointed task of bringing to light the bloodthirsty animals that prowled these streets. Alone or in feral packs, these monsters in human skin stalked the unsuspecting.

Below in the alleyway, four such animals crouched in ambush. Watching the flow of life in the more well lit thoroughfares, the young men barely stopped short of salivation as two scantily clad young women decided to take a dangerous shortcut home from a night of barhopping. One youth, obviously the leader, stepped out from the shadows. Smiling evilly at the women, he spoke with a boy's voice only weeks away from becoming a man's. Whether he made it through those weeks was up to chance. A really slim chance.

"You ladies have to pay a toll to come through here," grinned the tough evilly. "You musta forgot that this is Arachnid territory."

Backing away from the unexpected company, the two women did not notice the other gang members that appeared behind them. Bumping into the largest of the trio, the brunette gave a small scream and spun away from the sudden contact. The two remaining of the three stooges rushed to grab the women and quickly they were restrained. Vainly the women struggled but the creeps held them fast with greater than human strength.

I looked overhead and could see streaks of light as heroes flew to and fro, holding the night's evil at bay. They fought the good fight in a different way than me. They were gods and aliens and technological powerhouses. Speeding through the night's air, they hustled to stop this evil demon or that cunning supervillain. Me, I just stalked through the night searching for the very thing below me. I was just a simple guy who worked out a bit and wore some bulletproof armor. But my job was as tough as theirs. They could not be bothered to save two streetwalkers. I could. In fact, I prided myself on it.

Tendrils of dark light curled away from the eyes of the leader as he addressed the captives. A cold wind seemed to fill the dirty byway, blowing rubbish and stench. A web of otherworldly energy begun to spread through the alley. Darkness crept through the shadows, devouring the scant and sickly light. One of the stooges, a pink haired freakshow, holding the women could not keep his insanity in check and a sickening giggle slithered up from behind the blonde.

"I am sure you ladies think that some green or something else can get you out of this," snarled the head dude as he looked the women up and down, "but we need something a bit more dear. Your souls."

"Suck 'em dry. Start with this pretty, pretty one," giggled the freaky one, as he pushed the ashen and trembling woman at the boss thug.

"Shut it fool. I decide who gets harvested first, not you. Give me the other one. I can taste her lifeforce from here and it is delicious!" snapped the raven haired criminal.

The brunette was thrown at the hood's feet with a sob of pain and fear and disbelief. Free from the constrains of her captors, she failed to even attempt to run. Shock had set in and the two women were as good as dead. This was the part where it got bad for the wannabe super thugs. This was the part where I came in.

Crouched above the ambush, I had been waiting in the shadows. Watching the Arachnids set up their little trap, watching them argue over who gets the spoils for the night, watching them without them knowing it, I have been watching and waiting. Waiting for them to do something monumentally stupid, something like attempting to steal some relatively innocent people's souls in my neighborhood. Don't they teach these clowns anything in criminal school? Don't they know this is my turf? I always thought that the word about me had spread. It never ceased to amaze me when idiots like this waltzed into my ghetto.

Their red jackets rested in the pools of shadow like blood clots. The dark energies that gave them their power deepened the shadows and stretched the weak light until the alley was a surreal landscape. Hungrily, the black energy surged ahead. You could almost hear the souls of the devoured screaming for release as the energies reached out to the brunette hungrily. Well, there was no time like the present I supposed.

Grabbing the handle of the rusty fire escape, I vaunted over and dropped towards the leader. Knifing towards him like some sort of human bomb, I angled for the best way to greet the thug. Snapping a kick against the side of his head gave me the momentum to somersault into an attack position. I grinned and he grunted in pain and surprise.

"Welcome to the jungle!" I said. "We got fun and games." Cheesy, I know, but all the good lines are taken.

The boss staggered with the impact, not as much as I would like but still he staggered. His concentration broken by the sudden attack, his dark tendrils dissipated into the night. The women took this as a cue to snap out of their revelry and hurried to beat feet. One of the thugs, the tall one, turned tail and ran at the realization that this night's feeding would not be so worry free after all. The quiet one with the chrome dome and the cheap tats seemed to think he was some sort of powerhouse because he closed to me trying to grapple. A swift kick in the leg followed by a roundhouse kick to his face disabused him of any notions of grandeur. Guess his fight or flight instinct lead him wrong this time, it was always wise to choose flight when I'm around.

The crazy giggler pulled a knife and slashed at me while my back was turned. His blade slipped around my armor plates and cut, but not deeply. Even so it was painful. Spinning at the attack, I splattered blood on the alley walls where it turned black in the shadows. The giggler was grinning maniacally at the injury he caused. Slapping the knife away broke the crazy boy's hand but didn't seem to discourage him much. Leaping at my throat with his teeth bared, the giggler wasn't holding back. He seemed to think he was going to tear my throat out with his teeth. My fist eliminated any chances of his attack coming to fruition and padded some dentist's bill for the next few months. The whack's teeth clattered as they struck the filthy asphalt. The tooth fairy was gonna be busy at his house tonight. His hand covering the bleeding hole that was his giggle box, the crazy had finally had enough and turned tail. That left only the boss. His voice rang out behind me.

"Most impressive Mr. Spandex, most impressive," smiled the punk, a small trickle of blood lazily flowing from the side of his mouth, "but you will find that I am not so easily defeated."

"Get ready for a surprise, kid," I replied through clenched teeth. This would not be easy, the thug had shown that he was more than just a tough with a toy. He had some power in him to withstand that kick.

Throwing his hand at me, a dark stream lashed out from his splayed fingertips. I felt the chill wind and faintly heard a banshee's wail. Striking my Kevlar breastplate, the icy energy was mostly deflected but enough passed through to make me feel that I would never be warm again. A tiny gasp was all he got from me before I got hold of myself again, but even that was enough to send him into uncontrollable fits of manic laughter.

"Did you think you could just kick me and it would all be over with?" taunted the gang banger, "Did you really think that would be all it took? Did you really believe I was like all those others you fight?"

The small bit of dark energy that reached my body had leached enough of my lifeforce to make me slightly queasy and a little bit tired. My legs quivered and seemed to lack the power to remain standing. The thug, on the other hand, seemed energized by the siphoning of my energy and his slight wound was almost healed. My body hunched with aching and lingering pain, I stretched my trembling hand out towards the approaching youth.

Batting my hand away as if I were a child, the 'banger reached out and grabbed my vest. Lifting me off my feet without a hint of exertion, the thug spun and hurled me against the wall of the alleyway. My ribs cracked with the contact. The impact also shook my teeth in their sockets and caused my head to swim. Could you see those stars or was it just me?

An ugly face interrupted my dazed musings. Twisting his hand in my collar, the thug lifted me again. The cobwebs began to clear as the moonlight illuminated his evilly grinning countenance. I couldn't stand another impact like the one I just took. As it was, I could feel the ribs grinding in my chest. I could feel my teeth loosened from the impact. My head was spinning.

Dark energy once again curled and twisted and stretched out of the hood's eyes. Lust for death and hunger for power twisted his features into a repulsive caricature of the boy he should have been. Life, my life, began to drain away as the tough trembled at the exchange. Weakening, I slowly lifted my hands to my shoulders. Is this what molasses felt like? Why was I so tired? I just needed to sleep…

My eyes snapped open at the last thought. My training had taught me that the sleepy feeling meant I am about to die. I didn't want to die. Not tonight. Not now. My mind raced in fear. I was not used to this, the punks I usually faced did not posses such power.

Clapping my hands over the ears of my attacker, I grasped his lobes and one of his multitude of ear jewelry punched through my hand. But he took the worst of it when I violently shoved my thumbs into the gaping black pits that exist in place of his eyes.

A pained scream and coppery gushing of hot blood greeted my gambit and the hood dropped me. Landing somewhat gracefully on one knee, I knew I had to finish this quick. Launching myself at the hood, I tackled him as he was blindly walking away and gurgling some nonsense about not being able to see. It sounded like he was talking through one of those old time telephones with the crank. My grandfather had one of those. I could remember playing with it.

Shaking the cobwebs from my skull, I slammed the punk into the wall and grabbed the back of his head by his greasy filthy hair. A few swift slaps face-first into the bricks got the kid's attention, but did little to improve his looks.

"Surprise!" I said sarcastically as I delivered the finishing touch, a triple elbow to head, chest, and groin.

Spinning on the still standing criminal, I drew back my fist to finish him. I hesitated for one moment and the kid fell face first to the alley floor. Surveying the damage, I knew my back was still seeping blood, the hole in my hand hurt, and at least three of my ribs were broken. I dropped an emergency beacon on the toughs and stumbled back into the shadows to lick my wounds. The paddy wagon would be along shortly to pick up the Arachnids. And it was a good thing because I could barely pick up my own feet at the moment. Darkness fell.

I woke to the scurrying of rats and the hum of the beacon. The two toughs were still there, I had only been out a few moments, they would be out a lot longer. I seemed to have a concussion. Fumbling in my belt, I grabbed up a small vial of smelling salts. Cracking the glass, I inhaled deeply of the noxious fumes.

My eyes snapped open at the shocking stench. The salts would be what I needed to get to my lair. I needed to heal. After all, I was the Night Tiger and this was my Concrete Jungle. And tomorrow, the beasts would try to feed again. And then it was tomorrow.

Afternoon light filtered through the dusty blinds. Stabbing into my eyes, I groaned at the motes and beams infiltrating my slumber. I threw my arm over my face in hopes of grabbing a few more moments but it didn't work. As usual, once I was awake I needed to be up and moving. Sitting up in bed, the sheets twisted into knots around my legs, I could still feel the vertigo from last night and my ribs felt like a thousand midgets tap danced on them all night long. Damn midgets.

Untying the Gordian knot that held me in bed, I swung my legs onto the cold floor. Blinking sand out of my eyes, I surveyed the cramped and cluttered room that served as my lair. It was a small, three room apartment, the main room barely bigger than a bus stop. A dirty table stood across from my bed, empty liquor bottles littered it's surface like a wino's Taj Mahal. I started to rise but the dizziness returned with a vengeance and I found myself sinking back to the still warm bed. That punk and the vodka did a number on me last night, nothing that a little time, food, and advil can't cure. But still, I hurt. Well, time I had and advil was free from the infirmary at headquarters, but food was a different story. Maybe I would grab some ramen from that old guy down the street before heading to work. If I could hold it down, that is.

Finally getting hold of the swirling mess that was my equilibrium, I slowly rose and padded over to the dingy bathroom. I will keep my monologue to myself for a few minutes, thank you. After that business was taken care of, I slipped into the shower and let the tepid water wash away the last effects of sleeping off a nasty drunk. Toweling off, I felt almost human again.

Walking back into the broom closest that doubled as my bedroom, living room, and gym, I grabbed the tousled bed and flipped it up into it's wall recess. Underneath the bed rested a rubber mat patched with duct tape in several places. Pulling the well used mat into the center of the room, I began my daily regime of uncountable push-ups and sit-ups and stretching and generally sweating into the rubber. Those heroes with all the fancy powers did not know the dedication it took to be a hero in this city. To them, they were doing what was natural, to me it was more like self-induced torture everyday. Especially today.

Forcing myself to finish was harder than usual thanks to my screaming ribs and pounding head. However, I pushed through the pain and finish my daily masochism. Toweling off, I contemplated a quick hop back in the shower, but jumping on wet tiles is dangerous. Hehe, I guess I was still out of it today after all.

Three steps took me across the room to my closet. Opening the door, I pushed aside the handful of Salvation Army clothes to grab my spare uniform. The other would have to be dry-cleaned after my leisurely nap in the garbage last night. My uniform was black spandex with orange stripes, kevlar plates were strategically placed to protect anything really vital. Noticing a frayed edge, my finger located a hole in the fabric and relentlessly dug into it until pushing all the way through. Shaking my head at the imperfection in the expensive suit brought another way of nausea. Tossing the spare suit onto my raggedy recliner, I grabbed the roll of duct tape off the top shelf. Wrapping my ribs was a test of my pain tolerance and I nearly failed it. Wiping away the tears after finishing, I gingerly walked over to my waiting 'stume. Shoulda put off the workout today…

Struggling into my suit, I grabbed a heavy overcoat off the coat rack by the front door. I was late for my debriefing as it was but today was not going to be a day that I hurried. Tossing on the overcoat, I walked out of the door and down the hall to the stairwell. An old Out of Order sign decorated the beat up elevator door. Why couldn't I live in a building with a working elevator?

The stairwell smelled like piss, because drunk and fucked up people pissed in it. Never said I lived in the Ritz, you know. Being a non-super powered hero really didn't pay well in this city. While all licensed heroes are paid by the government and all heroes were equal, some heroes were more equal than others. I was one of the less fortunate.

I reached the bottom of the stairwell and only saw two rats, and only one was of the human variety. It could end up being a good day after all. The fat guy at the front desk noticed me immediately. I hated that guy, he reminded me of an angry and smelly Bookman from Good Times.

"Your rent is due on Thursday!" blubbered the fat guy, "No excuses this time, ya bum!"

"You'll get your money big man, don't sweat it. You'll get enough to buy one, maybe two lunches," I snarled in return.

I showed him my back as he gifted me with a few choice words. I was used to those types of gifts from people. Some heroes were greeted with flowers and some weren't. You could guess which type of hero I was. Reaching the filthy glass doors, I pushed through and into the hot street. A wall of noise and stench greeted me as I took in the urban squalor around me. To my left, homeless people camped out on a corner chastising people who really didn't have any spare change. There was no such thing as spare change in this neighborhood. To my right was a small cluster of desperate women wearing impossibly revealing outfits. A long white car rolled slowly past the intersection and the women turned their back on it. It was too early for this. I turned my back on their sad spectacle and trudged to the nearby tramway.

Sliding my security clearance through the pay slot saved me a quarter. Lucky for me, it was a quarter that I didn't have. I took the patriot line towards City Hall. As usual, I spent the time gazing out at the city I called home. Steel and glass fingers reached for the heavens alongside run down boroughs that were sliding into a hopeless version of hell. Technological wonders existed side by side with urban savagery. On my way, I saw dozens of heroes using their talents or toys or just plain grit to combat evil. Sadly, I also saw hundreds of instances of evil. No matter how many heroes reported for duty, there was always an unrelenting tide of villains for them to combat. And when I said unrelenting tide, I meant it.

Hundreds of small gangs existed in this city, and each had their own unique superpower or technology or magic or training with which to defend and control their turf. Occasionally they wouls ally with each other but usually they were fighting each other for the right to prey on the helpless herd. Alongside these gangs existed beings of unbelievable power and unlimited evil, Arch villains of the worst sort preyed upon the helpless denizens of my city. Archvillians who controlled legions of goons and constantly vied for what little prosperity and happiness this city could provide. My city.

Of course it wasn't mine, but when a man or woman laid their blood on the ground of a place to defend it they were allowed a little leeway. Once a person put their life on the line for an ideal, it was expected for them to believe in that ideal. But it still felt like it's my city. More than it felt that way for some indestructible demi-god swooping around from above while raining lightning, at least it seemed that way to me. Those guys weren't on the ground. They couldn't see the ravages that evil brought firsthand like I did. They didn't live in it. They flew above it untouched. They lived in skyscrapers and glass towers. They lived above us simple humans. They didn't live in the filth like I did. And I wouldn't change that even if I could.

A clanging bell signaled that my tram had reached it's destination. Heaving upright with a low groan, I limped slightly from my stiffening ribs. Exiting the tramway, I entered a much different version of my city than the one I had left. To my right, businessmen and women hurried in a pack across a busy street. I resisted the urge to bust a few yuppie jaywalkers and just looked to my left instead. There I saw a small park, well manicured, with a tiny horde of children cavorting on it's various amusements. Such a beautiful place, full of light...

But there was still darkness, I saw a small and dark alleyway near the park and I could literally feel the presence of crime to go with it's grime. Squinting slightly, I saw figures in the inky black and knew that my hunch was correct. Maybe, I would tell Straight Arrow or American Jihad to check it out. Maybe I wouldn't.

Who was I kidding? I would tell them. I wouldn't be able to live with myself if any of these unsuspecting people were hurt.

Crossing at the corner, I got my morning view of City Hall. In my city, City Hall was one of the most magnificent buildings. Marble columns flecked with gold surrounded an immense and beautiful courtyard. Tall statues honored fallen heroes and other, more regular people who sacrificed for the good of all. Colored fountains sprayed into the sky, as people lounged around enjoying the tranquility. The building itself was a monstrosity and yet still was pleasing to view. Iambic columns held up the vast white overhang and gave the marble and brick building a stately appearance. Heroes stood guard around the plaza and on the roof of the Hall. Flying in patterns over the area, other heroes warily scanned for any suspicious activity. Few villains were dumb enough to attack City Hall.

Walking past the assembled citizens, I could feel their gazes and vaguely hear their whispers. Sadistic, they said. Unwarranted violence, came the whispers in the wind. Distrustful gazes followed me to the entrance of the building. I always found it funny that nobody had anything to say when some of the more powerful heroes unleashed their might but let me slap around a few thugs and people were afraid of me. Like I said, funny.

The door shuts out the morning light and my eyes quickly adjusted to the much dimmer atrium. The Bubbler was working the booking desk. Arrayed in the line of chairs beside the desk sat a handful of morose criminals enclosed in clear bubbles of pure energy. One seemed to be throwing a temper tantrum and you could almost feel the heat coming off the inferno incased in a force field.

"Been like that all day?" I asked Bubbles, gesturing to the raging blaze.

"Yep, and it is only one o'clock. The idiot over there will burn himself out soon enough though. He is quickly running out of oxygen," returned the Bubbler with a grin.

"Ha! If they were smart they wouldn't be criminals!" I replied as I walk past the desk.

Reaching the time clock, I punched in. Turning, I checked my in-box and saw that I was to report to debriefing room 12 to give my account of last night and to receive my new assignment. Crumpling up the memo, I filed it in the garbage can. Where the hell was debriefing room 12 anyway?

I just went to my desk instead. If they really wanted me, they would send someone for me. No sooner had I had that thought than a ghostly figure appeared next to my chair. The figure had a vague representation of a superhero costume and whitish tendrils snaking away from it's form.

"Whatcha want, Shimmer?" I asked the wispy figure.

"You are late for your meeting Tiger," came the ghostly echo of a voice, "I was sent to escort you. The bosses seem to think you don't know where the debriefing room is."

"Well, for once they are right. Lead on!" I shot back as I stood.

I followed Shimmer through the room and down deep into the bowels of the building. I liked Shimmer. He wasn't all that bad, for a dead guy that is. Shimmer was one of the city's oldest heroes. He had the ability to turn ghostly and intangible. One night some old enemies of his snuck into his bedroom and slit his throat. He woke up dead, but still came to work. Now that was dedication to your job!

"Have fun in there and keep your head up," advised Shimmer with humorous intent as we reached a door marked with the number 12.

"Sure thing, Shimmer." I replied, "You might want to have a bite to eat, you are looking a bit peaked today."

Shimmer grinned at the jest as he glided off to his next errand. I, on the other hand, had little to grin about as I pushed open the door into the debriefing room. Inside the room was my supervisor, Thunderclap, two costumed heroes I did not know and a suit. The two heroes were quietly seated to the side of the room, while Thunder and the suit occupied the far side of the interview table. Nobody rose when I entered. Who did I have to slap to get some respect around here?

"Have a seat Night Tiger," flatly said the suit.

They obviously had studied me. It's obvious because they were taken aback when I actually grinned and sat in the awaiting chair as opposed to what my files say would be my usual response. Something like "Go fuck yourself" or maybe something a bit less nice. And usually the files would have been correct, but today I hurt too damn much to be my normally rebellious self.

With a nod from the suit, Thunderclap launched into his same old tirade about excessive violence and how I am giving the department an image problem. I countered his speech with my usual tactic. I closed my eyes and blocked out his voice. Eventually, and it seemed like an eternity, he wrapped it up and I could finally bring my attention back to the conversation. Thunderclap looked over to the suit and signaled that he was finished.

"What do you think of all that, Night Tiger?" asked the suit impassively.

"I think of it the same way I always do," I replied, "I think it is fucking bullshit. There is a war zone out there away from the pretty lights and fancy people. Spend one week on my beat and you will understand that I am actually taking it easy on these animals."

Thunderclap's facial expression was worth whatever punishment my response receives. His mouth dropped open and his eyes widened. His face became as red as Flaming Demon's. You could tell that he was about to burst into a screaming fit and maybe fire me when the suit began talking.

"I agree," said the suit, "that is why you're here."

This time it was my turn to have the priceless expression. It was the first time that someone in any position of authority had agreed with my assessment of the less than perfect areas of the city. I was speechless as he continued.

"We need more people like you on the streets." said the suit, "We are interested in you because you work the toughest beat in the city and you have no superpowers to back you up. Just your own will and determination. The gang banger, named Darkfall, you nailed last night has already put a half dozen superheroes in the hospital. You took him out with nothing but your head, hands, and feet. And that is impressive."

"Well, to be honest, luck had a lot to do with it," I grinned sheepishly, unaccustomed as I was to praise.

"Luck or not, you get results. That is why we are asking you to join up with us to finish the Darkfall case," countered the suit, dismissing my remark.

"Okay, I'm listening," I said.

The suit began a long winded speech about this evil guy, and that gang of thugs and this vile scheme, and that dastardly plan. When it was all over, I found out that the suit's name was Mediator and his two spandex friends were Guardian Angel and Primal Force. I found out that someone or some group was trying to unite the various gangs in the city under one leader. And whoever it was, they were good at what they did. Supposedly nobody had any clue to their identity. The most reliable reports implied that a handful of powered supervillians named the Shadow Chamber may have been responsible. The Shadow Chamber was legend and lore among do-gooders. I had always dismissed them as a bedtime story for heroes. I found out that there had been a major upswing in violence and criminal activity in the city this month. I already knew things had gotten rough in my area but I had no idea that it had spread to all quadrants of the city. Immediately, the figures in the alleyway outside City Hall came to mind. I openned my mouth to alert Thunder Clap when the suit chimed in again.

"We have already dispatched American Jihad to handle the Hellfires in the alleyway." interjected Mediator, "I gleaned the information from your surface thoughts when you entered the building."

"Stay outta my head, chief," I said as my brows furrowed in anger at the intrusion, "or there will be trouble."

"No offense, Tiger. I usually refrain from listening in on people's minds and yours is usually strong." explained the suit hastily, "You were broadcasting that thought all the way from the tram. It is hard not to hear surface things when I am concentrating on the person having those thoughts. My apologies."

"Whatever," I replied flatly, "just stay out."

"Well, wrapping up, I have knowledge that a major meeting is taking place in the Aztec district. You three should go break it up. Primal knows the address," supplied Mediator.

At that, the debriefing was over and we all filed out into the hall. Mediator and Thunderclap walked off deeper into the bowels of the building. Me and the two capes turned towards the stairwell and our mission.

"I don't usually work with partners," I explained, "so you may have to forgive any anti-social behavior I exhibit."

"Don't worry," replied Angel, a pretty woman in a white and blue jumpsuit, "I play well with others."

A grunt and a nod from Primal signaled that he heard me and I suppose I couldn't ask for more. The three of us eventually reached ground level and stepped out into the bright sunshine. Looking to Primal, he pointed towards the tramway and said one word. "Central"

I took it to mean that he wanted us to take the central tram line. Which was fine by me, that meant the mission was near my apartment. I began to trot towards the tram when a strange thing happened. Suddenly I lifted off the ground and began to speed across the courtyard. Looking around in confusion I saw that Angel had a funny look on her face and all of us were flying in a glowing nimbus of white energy.

"Not to alarm you, but it is quicker this way." she grinned through clenched teeth, "But it takes a lot of concentration so I don't so it that often."

"Well, by all means, keep concentrating," I replied nervously as I watched the ground speed past way below us. I hate flying.

Quickly we arrived at the tramway, Angel was true to her word. We landed with a soft thump that still hurt my aching ribs. Seeing my grimace, Angel raised her left hand an a soft blue light covered me. Instantly the pain in my ribs subsided, the hole in my hand closed, and the scratch on my back stopped irritating me.

"Next time, tell me you are hurt!" said Angel as she shook her head, "What good is a healing ability if nobody tells you when they need it?"

"Thanks lady, I will," I grinned, "next time."

We boarded the central line and the journey wass uneventful. I passed my time as I always did, watching my city speed past. Soon we were off the tram and huffing it through the nearly deserted streets of the Aztec district. Bright banners flapped in the breeze, enticing nobody. A lone cat scurried across the empty street and into the shadows under a dumpster. The businesses were closed and apartment windows were shut off from the world. My mind's eye could see that tumbleweeds wouldn't be out of place here.

"Where is everyone?" asked Primal. "This place is a ghost town."

The surreal neighborhood blunted any amazement at the statement from Primal, the longest he had spoken yet. Moving on quiet feet, we all felt eyes upon us. Crossing the street and moving down the block we approached the warehouse where this meeting was supposed to take place. Stopping in an alley near the building, we surveyed the area and noted several guards. They would be my job.

Leaving the two capes behind, I slipped behind the first of the sentries. One punch in the back of the head gives him some much needed beauty sleep. Moving on to the next and the next, eventually all the thugs were dreaming of sugar plum fairies. It was easy when they were too worried about how they looked or who they were impressing. Sliding quietly back to my team, I startled Angel with my silent approach.

"Don't do that!" she nearly screamed when I touched her shoulder. "I could have blasted you."

"Promises, Promises." I replied with a slightly sarcastic grin. "Besides, I would have dodged."

"Take care of them all?" asked Primal gruffly.

"Try to keep it down, chatterbox." I returned. "I got 'em"

"Then lets go." said Primal, obviously not a person with much of a sense of humor.

We moved as a group towards the entrance of the warehouse. Primal gripped the locked doorknob and simply twisted the door off it's hinges. I rushed in first, don't ask me why. Angel and Primal followed. Quickly my eyes adjusted to the dark of the, until recently, abandoned building. Angel and Primal both had protection from most things that would kill little old me. Angel could heal herself and Primal was almost indestructible. I had to just be better than whatever criminals threw at me. For that reason, I slipped away from the two super powered heroes and let my senses extend. Before my companions could realize that I was no longer with them, I had already pinpointed several people moving around and talking quietly in a back room. Slipping back behind my teammates, I decided to wait until they saw me. No reason to make Angel scream again with bad guys in the vicinity. It took a minute before Primal wondered where I was.

"Tiger?" asked the big hero.

"Here." I whispered. "There are upwards of a dozen people in the room on the left"

I pointed towards the back left side of the building and we all snuck as silently as possible towards the gathering of criminals. Angel and I took up positions on either side of the closed door as Primal stepped up and grabbed the knob silently. Angel caught my eye and held up three fingers. I nodded in agreement. Then she was holding two fingers…then one…

Primal's arm flexed and the metal door screamed off it's hinges. I leapt through the open doorway and snap kicked the tough standing to my right. He doubled over in pain and I followed through with a perfectly placed punch to his right cheek. Before his unconscious body hit the ground, I was already moving towards my next target. The steel door came flying through the portal and took out two hoods with a clang. Primal stepped through the open doorway and let out a roaring challenge. Most of the villains turned towards the sound and motion, which gave me room to smack down two more gimps. Angel slid into the room and unleashed bright white flashes of energy that served to confuse and blind many of the assembled villains. Within moments, most of the henchmen were down and the three of us turned towards the two figures standing in the center of the room.

Both were clad in gang colors, nothing unusual about that in this city. What was unusual about it was the fact they are rival gangs. Scimitar, leader of the Blades, and Cloudburst, leader of the

Weathermen, glanced at each other and grinned. Scimitar reached over his shoulder and pulled out an immense flaming lava sword, while Cloudburst threw his hands above his head and the room instantly goes from a sweltering 90 degrees to a blisteringly cold 20 degrees.

Shivering in my spandex, I rushed at the sword wielding maniac as Angel hurled flashes of light at Cloudburst. Out of the corner of my eye, I saw Primal slowly moving toward Cloudburst as well. Seemed cold didn't suit him that well. As I neared Scimitar, I checked my headlong rush. Lucky for me that I did because the flaming sword sliced through the air where my head would have been had I kept going. Quickly stepping into his space before he can check his backswing, I grabbed the tough's wrist. A bit of leverage disarmed the warrior and a hard punch in the gut made him double over in pain.

"A flaming sword ain't much help if you can't hold onto it," I grinned sarcastically.

A swift elbow sent the Blade leader into a restless slumber on very cold concrete. Speaking of cold, I spun to assist my companions with Cloudburst but two standing heroes and one unconscious villain were all the proof I needed that this meeting is over.

We waited until the collection team arrived to carry the criminals to the Tower. Then we went our separate ways until tomorrow, my teammates went back to whatever wonderland they live in and I trudged a couple of blocks over until I entered my turf. My Concrete Jungle.

On familiar territory, my whole attitude changed. My walk became more of a prowl and my senses sharpened to a painful point. I could smell the rotting garbage and sad despair that permeated my stomping grounds. I could feel the insidiously creeping evil that only villains gave an area. I could see every inch of sad decay and dashed hopes. I could hear the melancholy whispers of broken dreams. I could taste the hate. Mediator was right, there was an upswing of criminal behavior throughout my whole city.

Watching the foot traffic from my hidden alcove in an alleyway, I noticed the two girls I rescued last night beginning their nightly hunt for degradation. I could see them displaying their assets to passing cars. A dirty white sedan pulled up and the blonde hustled over and hopped in. As the car sped away, the brunette looked up and actually noticed me from my hiding spot. Looking both ways, she crossed the sparsely populated street. She was headed straight for me.

"Hey." She said nervously. "I…I just wanted to thank you. Nobody has ever stood up for me before without asking for anything in return."

"Who says I don't want something in return?" I replied in a steely voice.

"Well, I will do whatever you want." she said flatly with hooded eyes.

Her attitude had changed in an instant and the world weary side had taken over. Obviously she had something in mind to use as repayment. Just not what I had in mind.

"What is your name, child?" I asked with a bit of disarming concern.

"Honey," she said with a short voice devoid of real feeling.

"Nice name." I nodded. "What is your real one?"

"I…Michelle," she admited.

"Why are you out here Michelle?" I asked. "Why do you do this to yourself?"

"Because I have no choice, because I have a child to feed and mother dying of cancer and I have no other options," she said with obvious desperation.

"What do you make a night?" I asked.

"About $150 dollars," she replied sadly, "and even that is not enough."

"Well, I do want something in return for saving you." I finally said after scrutinizing the girl for a moment. "Several things actually. First, I want you to take this money, get you some food, a toy for your kid, and go home for the night." I said as I pressed two crumpled hundred dollar bills in her hand. "Second, I do not want to see you out here doing this ever again."

"I can't take this," she said as she attempted to return the money.

"Yes, you can. You owe me." I replied with a much harder voice. Softening a bit, I hand her a business card. "Take this to the address on the card at ten o'clock tomorrow morning. Ask for Charley, she will give you a job that pays around eleven hundred a week plus benefits. It is drudge work, typing and filing and answering the phone."

That being said, I turned and melted into the shadows of the alleyway while Michelle read the card. My whisper floated back to her ears, "But it's honest." And her reply reached my straining ears, "Thank you, Night Tiger."

It was my rent money. My last two bills, but something would come up I suppose. If I could save just one of those women then maybe I could make up for not saving my mother the same way. She also had been a woman of the night. The night had taken her innocence, then her youth, then her beauty, then her self respect, and finally her life. Few knew it, but that was why I am out here every time the sun goes down. To take back from the night what it had taken from me.

Perching on an overhanging ledge, I noticed some thugs strutting down the street in broad moonlight. They moved with false bravado, swaggering and preening but with a furtive gleam to their eyes and a sheen of perspiration in the relatively cool evening. Who did these punks think they are these days?

While my section of the city was far from a paradise, unless you mean Dante's, crime was not as rampant here as elsewhere. I would like to say that was my fault but it was probably just the creeping malaise of this place. It was hard to get motivated to do anything with decaying squalor surrounding you. It was hard to do anything with such sorrow around, even break the law.

The pack of hoods stopped in front of an abandoned building. Once it had been a clothing store but that was back when people in this neighborhood knew window shopping as more than an urban legend. One of the bad guys stood as lookout and another bent to pick the lock on the old glass doors. Minutes passed and still the old lock withstood the young punk's endeavors. Finally, one of the older and bigger punks pushed the lock picker aside and simply punched the door open.

"Open Sesame." snarled the 'banger as he made a chopping motion to his assembled crew. "Get in there!"

They hustled through the door and it swung shut behind them. All in all the operation had taken about 4 minutes. Half a dozen guys and it took them 4 minutes to open an old door and even then they had to break it. It was about fucking time, gimps.

I was worried that some other hero would chance along and stumble into the trap they were setting for me. Oh, yes, I knew it was a trap. I figured that out moments after seeing them for the first time. They were the bait. Something in that old store was the teeth of the trap. Well, why wait around?

Reaching down I grasped the concrete ledge and swung out into space. Calculating my swing, I let go and felt gravity wrap it's uncaring arms around me. But my aim was true and I was able to hook my fingertips into the pipe running down the side of the building. Moving hand over hand, I quickly descended to the ground and in seconds was at the broken front door.

Now I was faced with a dilemma like the one faced by the little bald guy in the Princess Bride. For some reason I loved that movie. Anyway, did I assume that the person setting up this trap thinks I am dumb or did I guess that this person thinks I am smart? I know, it's confusing to me too.

I decided to take the third option. I would do something that the person setting up this trap would never expect. I called for help.

Twenty minutes later, Primal and Angel showed up and the three of us walked into the broken front door. We burst into the front of the building like gangbusters. Well, we were technically gangbusters after all. We were uneventfully welcomed by an empty room unless you counted a sneezing fit from Angel when she was attacked by vicious dust bunnies.

"Spread out and be on your toes," I whispered.

The three of us took different doors and as luck would have it, my door turned out to be the prize. Behind the thin plywood, I heard whispered voices and trembling breaths. I smelled perspiration intermingled with fear. I tasted someone's cologne in the air, it was cheap whatever it was. I felt the heat from the doorknob that told me someone touched it recently. I saw the dust disturbed at the base of the door. Even though it may seem like I did, I didn't have super powers. I simply had spent many years at the feet of a martial arts master. He had taught me to stretch out my senses and to become like the stalking tiger. He had made me able to see the tiny changes in the world that most leave in their passing. He enabled me to move in silence and hide in shadows, to anticipate my prey and lie in wait for them.

This time something was wrong. I could see all the signs but there was something else there. Something that I should have known but did not, something I should have seen but refuse too danced right on the edges of my mind. There was something missing in the 'bangers tracks. That was the only way I could describe it, something lacking. Whatever.

I gave the signal and Primal smashed through the door like he had a grudge against it. He leapt into a room with a few empty boxes and a dozen thugs with weapons drawn. However, a six and a half foot tall, 280 pound monster of a hero is not what they had expected. They'd expected little old me.

Well, so that none of them felt put out, I leapt into the room and grabbed the two closest hoodlums by the back of their heads. The look on their faces was classic.

"Hey Moe!" I taunted as I smacked their heads together with a satisfying crunch.

Spinning away from Larry and Curly, I punched one particularly ugly kid as Angel entered the room throwing her flashy stuff. One of the 'bangers that had thought he was sneaking up on me with a tire iron was an unfortunate recipient of Angel's flash and howled in fear as his sight deserted him.

"Thanks, but I knew he was there." I grinned at Angel as I launched a particularly nasty ridge hand at a fleeing villain.

"You're welcome." returned Angel. "I think!"

Across the room, Primal was wrapping up the last of the punks. With powerful, bone crunching punches and literal disdain for the attacks the surrounding enemies, Primal simply knocked out a punk with each swing. Within the blink of an eye he had taken out seven opponents.

"You called us out for this?" chided Primal with the first humor he has shown. "I have tougher workouts signing autographs in playgrounds."

I started to reply with some extremely sarcastic and intelligent comment like "Shut up" or "Bite me" when that feeling of nothing that should be something returned. Something was wrong and the hair on my arms stood on end. Dropping into a crouch, I slowly turned to survey the room. I passed over the open doorway, I had already heard the two people outside. One was male and seemed familiar and the other was female with a light tread and expensive perfume. They were not the thing that had me on edge.

"See?" I replied to Primal. "You get what you ask for."

Primal and Angel spun around to the open door as to two villains stepped into the room. The female was dressed in black armor and leather that barely covered enough of her to even keep me from blushing. A black glow seemed to emanate from her dark eyes and a snide smile crossed her regal features. The other villain was a bit more familiar.

"Don't act so surprised!" sarcastically said Mediator. "It doesn't become you."

"But…You're a hero." stammered Primal as Angel regarded the black clad woman. "You are a good guy."

"Obviously not." declared the woman. "Just be done with them Mediator. They are peasants."

"Patience, my dear, this just wouldn't be right without a soliloquy." he replied. Turning to us, he says "I am sure you are wondering who my companion is. She is known as Shadow Queen and has control over energies from a dimension devoid of light. She is here for Guardian Angel."

"And I intend to devour her and use her light to feed my shadows." smiled Shadow Queen, looking like nothing more than a hungry shark. "You will keep them happy for days, my little glowing Angel."

Angel turned to me and Primal with full fledged terror in her face. I winked at her and addressed the two villains.

"That is a great plan," I smiled, "I see just one problem with it. There are two of you and three of us."

"Oh, have no fear, I can handle Primal with little more than a furrowing of my brow." confidently said Mediator. "For all his strength and indestructible body, his mind is weak."

"You forgot about me, fancy man." I grinned. "Your little mind tricks won't even give me a headache."

"You are correct, your mind is far from weak," laughed Mediator, "but who said I forgot about you?"

WRONG! Something was wrong, something I should have known. It was there, in my mind. I knew it before I heard a cruel voice snaked out from the shadows beside me. My heart froze in my chest.

"Hello brother." whispered White Crane with malice. "Remember me?"

My mind reeled. I was young. Maybe fourteen, it was a few years after my mother was taken by the night. I was with the Master. He was teaching me and three other children. On my left was Morgan, who became known as Monkey Paw and was killed in battle with a giant robot. On my right was Jeff, who operated under the name Cobra and was murdered by a powerhouse super villain named Battlefield. Behind me was Kaya, the only female in the class, who later was known as White Crane and supposedly died in a car wreck. We all had taken names after the fighting style we learned. I studied tiger style, Morgan studied monkey style, Jeff studied snake style, and Kaya studied crane style. The Master taught us each according the our body type. Each student was a match for any other student.

"You are dead, Crane." I replied. "One way or another, it doesn't matter to me."

My bravado convinced nobody. Not even me. With a snide grin, Mediator pointed his finger at us.

"Kill them."

Black shadow reached across the room and surrounded Angel who tried to beat it back with her light. A bright glow appeared around her and held the flood of dark at bay, but she wouldn't last for long. Mediator raised his hand to his temple and his eyes seemed to lose focus. Across the room, Primal dropped to his knees in mid-stride. Screaming in agony and holding his head, Primal Force appeared down for the count. I leapt backwards as Crane flew at me with her characteristic flurry of kicks. I savagely blocked the final kicks and launched into a rapid succession of powerful kicks and clawing hand strikes. She spun and flipped and dodged my attacks. Dropping into a fighting stance, both of us grinned at each other.

"Just like old times, Marvin," taunted White Crane.

"Don't call me Marvin, bitch," I replied with a grimace.

Without a single twitch of warning, she leapt the distance dividing us. A powerful fist filled my vision and for a split second I swore I could count the tiles in the ceiling. Spinning from the follow up attack that I knew was coming, I swept out with my leg and cut Crane's legs from under her. Staggering back, I attempted to clear the cobwebs as she flipped to her feet with casual disdain. She looked at me with nothing but hate and pain in her eyes.

"You were the Master's favorite." she sneered. "I SHOULD HAVE BEEN!"

With malice, she slowly stalked towards me. That was when I had what some would call an epiphany. I knew what to do. Screwing my face up with what I hope appeared as fear, I continued to back away from my advancing nemesis.

Forcing a tremble in my voice, I said "Please Kaya…don't do this."

"Yes, beg for your worthless life," she smiled hatefully, "not that it will matter."

Finally I had backed into the place I wish to be. I stood upright with a firm back and looked Crane in the eye. She stopped in her tracks and stared back at me with hate and madness in her face.

"Then do your worst," I said with a proud voice, "kill me, but I will forever be more loved by him than you ever were. I will not fight you."

Rage flared in her eyes and with a throat splitting scream, she launched at me with a killing blow. Time slowed for me as her hand knifed towards my heart. Madness gripped her face and spittle was slipping from the corner of her mouth as she put all her power into a death strike. A slightly cruel smile twisted my lips as I gave her my chest as a target.

She forgot the most important lesson taught to us. It wasn't the fighting style. It wasn't how strong you were, or how fast. It was how smart you are. It was how much you paid attention to yourself and your surroundings. As her body reached the point of perfection in motion, I dropped to the floor.

Almost comical surprise marked her face as she flew past me. The path of her strike sent her into the tidal wave of shadow menacing Angel. Screaming, she was enveloped in the murk and the horrible sound of feeding came from inside. Shadow Queen was gripped in the pleasure of drinking Crane's light and could not defend herself against Angel's right cross.

Across the room, Primal had almost risen to his feet. His effort was taking a toll. Blood poured from his nostrils and ears and pain had etched his face. His voice scratched and broken from screaming, he rasped with each sawing breath. But he was standing and trying to move toward Mediator. Why the hell not help the fellow out?

I stepped over and punched the slight villain in the side of the head. Mediator dropped like a rock. Looking around the room, nobody was in any mood to party. Angel looked ashen and afraid. Primal had collapsed in a heap of sobbing superhero. I caught my reflection in a grimy window and I didn't recognize my face. Was that me?

I dropped a beacon as Angel came out of her revelry and began to heal our physical wounds. What she could not heal was our hearts and heads. Somebody out there wanted us dead and it had almost happened. Somebody out there wanted us out of the way.

Life in the Concrete Jungle was simple. You were either predator or prey. It couldn't get simpler than that. Sometimes it could mean you were a bit of both too. Tonight was a perfect example, we were both predator and prey all wrapped up in spandex. This city made a habit of throwing curveballs at a person. You either learned to hit 'em or you ended up striking out.

The collection team arrived and packed up the unconscious villains. Initial reports were filed and the three of us were free to leave. A dejected Primal Force wearily trudged off to the nearby tramway. Angel and I spent a few minutes making idle chit chat and then headed our separate ways.

Being that I was already in my neighborhood, I decided to the long way home. Checking all the hotspots in the blanket of night, I finally had to accept that this was one of those infrequent quiet evenings and decided to head home.

The encounter with White Crane had shaken me to my very core. The next thing I knew I was sitting at my rundown kitchen table with a half empty bottle of cheap whiskey. The bottle was calling to me, if I strained my ears I could hear it's siren song. No, you are stronger than this.

Then the bottle was quarter empty and the siren was a funeral dirge. The morose trumpeting of a marionette's burial parade, the wailing of a widowed woman and I found it to be fucking irresistible. Maybe I wasn't so strong after all.

Revelations and Stuff

"Revelations come when you're in the thick of it,
pitting yourself up against something larger than yourself."
—Frank Langella, actor

The sun awoke me with the pain of a very much warranted hangover. As was my habit, I had fallen off the wagon once again. And all it had taken was an old enemy who had faked her own death and hidden for years for the simple chance to kill me. Never said I wasn't complicated.

My waking rituals taken care off and the last effects of a night of power drinking behind me, I suited up and headed out to work. The fat guy at the counter tried to remind me that my rent was due tomorrow and I just walked past him without acknowledging his even speaking. The usual suspects were all out in force today, panhandling and soliciting. I ignored them as I stalked to the tramway. My instincts were telling me that I was missing something. Just like my picking up on Crane's presence, even if I couldn't pinpoint the feeling, I was picking up on something else that danced around the edge of my head. Whatever it was, my brain would eventually tear at it until the thought floated to the top.

Watching the city pass by in the window did not hold the allure it usually does. To tell the truth, it no longer felt as much like my city. It no longer seemed like I remembered. That somebody out there would want me out of the picture and so effectively and perfectly acquire an enemy capable of doing it was kind of scary. Whoever was responsible was a mastermind and without anything else to go on, I was going to have no chance of catching them. I would have to wait for them to try to kill me again and hope that I could beat the odds once more. Why me?

The question had been floating around since the minute last night that I sniffed out the ambush being set for me. What was so important about me anyway? I was just a guy who dukes it our with common street thugs. Targeting Primal made a lot more sense. He was a powerhouse. Angel being a target made about as much sense as me being one. Why try to kill a healer? Way too complicated for a head breaker like me.

The only thing that was for sure was that I needed to find out more about this conspiracy theory that I blocked out earlier, and for that I needed Angel and Primal again. Getting Angel to agree to meet once again was easy, Primal was a different story. He seemed to feel that with Mediator locked up, the case was closed. I disabused him of that silly idea by pointing out the larger conspiracy and the thorough and deadly tactics being brought against us. I convinced him that he was safer with us than by himself.

The two of them and I met in a secluded coffee shop for a donut and brainstorming. I pushed and prodded them to squeeze every last tidbit about this group of villains pulling strings behind the scene. I found out that they were called the Shadow Chamber and most super villains were well aware of their existence if not too knowledgeable about anything else having to do with them. It seemed that this group had been around for decades, morphing from form to form and changing it's membership to match the times. However, enough was known about them to speculate about their involvement in most major criminal plots in the city over the past few decades. Some theorize that they go back as far as recorded history, playing games and generally causing mayhem. The one constant with the Chamber was the background manipulation of my city and the murder of many of it's defenders and citizens. Any hero that got too close to the Shadow Chamber ended up wearing cement shoes or some other tacky way to die like waking up with your throat cut. Were you thinking what I was thinking?

Leaving the coffee shop and my companions behind, I hurried over to City Hall to speak with Shimmer. Finally tracking him down in the depths of the building, I immediately begin berating him for information.

"Give with the goods, Shimmer." I demanded. "What can you tell me about the Shadow Chamber?"

"Good afternoon to you too, Tiger." he replied in sepulchral tones. "You are very impatient today."

"The Shadow Chamber, Shimmer," I repeated.

"Are they still around after all these years?" Shimmer pondered. "They were the last case I was working on before my old enemies tracked me down and murdered me."

"I know." I replied. "I was working on a case involving the Shadow Chamber and an old enemy of mine came back from the dead and tried to kill me. Sound familiar?"

"Indeed it does. Until now I had not thought to connect the Shadow Chamber with my death." he said. "Well, as I remember it, the Shadow Chamber consisted of seven powerful and immortal arch villains. One of the secrets of the Chamber is that it doesn't recruit new members, the original villains simply change identities every few years."

"Great, just what I need, a battle royal with a group of gods," I lamented sarcastically.

Smiling slightly at my tone, Shimmer continued. "Let's see, there was Aurora, mistress of light and Damia, summoner of darkness. There was Glacier, with powers over cold and Lava Storm, master of magma, and flame. Brainpain was a psychic powerhouse and Rock Crusher was one of the strongest villains in recorded history. The last was only known as the Dark Leader. He controlled the Chamber."

Gliding away, Shimmer glanced back for a moment, "One more thing, these days they will be going by different names. All the villains I just detailed were thought killed in the 80s. Very few living understand that all these villains are still around today, living hidden lives. They don't even know who each other are. They keep their various incarnations secret from even each other, that is how they can keep existing in a world of super heroes."

"Shimmer!" I called out to the retreating apparition. "Why haven't you mentioned this before?'

"You never asked," replied the ghost with a puzzled tone, "I am dead, remember?"

My concrete jungle was rarely a quiet place. Tonight was no different. Hungry predators stalked the shadows, yearning for prey. The prey, for all it's caution, had no real idea of the danger it faced on all sides. As the night deepened, the desire of the predators grew and the vigilance of the prey lessened. As the moon waned, the evil expanded. There would always be predators and prey in the concrete jungle.

The old couple only wanted to get home from the church bingo in time to watch Letterman. They were not watching for predators, their only concern was tonight's game.

"That Sophia is cheating." complained Barbara. "She always comes in first or second."

"And you always come in second or third, sweetie." replied John, hoping to avoid an argument. "But if you think she is cheating then say something to the reverend."

"You know I can't do that," countered the woman, "I have no proof that she's cheating."

Unnoticed by the bingo lady and her henpecked husband, a group of youth toughs were lounging in the darkened stairwell they just walked past. I noticed them earlier and I saw their ears perk up at the mention of Babs winning at bingo. As the couple pass, the hoods quietly slipped out of the shadow and began to silently stalk them. Up the block was an area where several street lights are broken or burned out. That was where the punks would make their move.

I leapt across the space between the roof I was on and the one next to me. Landing lightly, I sprinted across the room with a whisper of fabric chasing my movement. Another blind faith leap carried me to the building I wanted. I quickly hustled over to the fire escape and descended to a safe height to jump from. A couple of stories off the ground, I leapt out into space and bounded off the wall across the alley. Using the contact with the grimy bricks to slow my fall, I softly landed on the filthy pavement. Gliding through the alley brings me to the edge of the street, where I observed the gang bangers quickening their pace to coincide with the elderly couple entering the pool of shadow.

I slid around the corner of the building. Quickly sprinting across the street, I fell in behind the thugs. The old folks stepped into the shadow and the punks made their move. Grabbing the couple and forcing them against the wall caused the man to gasp and the woman to scream.

"Scream all you want!" sneered one of the bangers. "Nobody will help you now."

Damn, and I thought I was cheesy. It just goes to show that no matter how good you think you are, there was always someone better.

"Guess that means you think I am a nobody." I grinned. "That really hurts my feelings."

Spinning at the sound of my voice, the toughs forgot their prey and moved to surround me. There were only four of them, this would hardly be a workout. One of the gimps decided to charge me, a simple front kick doubled him over ending his lunge. That left three, they moved in a pack at me. Leaping at the center criminal, I kicked him in the face. Using his chin as a springboard, I split my legs to land a kick on the faces of the remaining two. Then there were none. Four opponents defeated in seven seconds. I should be paid by the criminal as opposed to getting salary. What we need was a free market superhero economy.

Dropping a beacon on the sleeping beauties, I motioned to the elderly couple. They were shaken and a bit scared but okay. Walking over to them, I bent to pick up grandma's pocketbook.

"Here you go, lady." I smiled. "If you don't mind, I will escort you home."

"We would like that Night Tiger." supplied John. "Thank you so much for being there for us."

Walking the old couple home took about ten minutes but it was time well spent. They told me of the way things used to be here. How the city used to be a bit rough but still had a magical appeal to it. They complained at the passing of that feeling and it's being replaced with the melancholy and hopelessness that lives here now.

I couldn't agree more. Sometimes I wondered why I fought so hard every night. Then I would meet someone like John and Barbara, they helped to keep me focused on why I did it. We finally arrived at their apartment building and Barbara tried to make me take her winnings for the night. It's twenty bucks that I could have used but it was money they needed. One of these days, I was going to have to start rolling these punks that I busted. Just one of them could finance all sorts of good projects in my neighborhood. Projects like Food for Poor Superheroes or the Night Tiger Rent Fund. Nah, if I did that I would have to arrest myself.

When the moon set over the concrete jungle, most of the jungle's denizens slept. Even predators get tired. I know I did. There was a new bottle of whiskey on my table. I didn't know how it got here but it was here now and that was all that mattered. Part of me blanched at the thought of the fiery liquid burning down my throat, sadly more of me wondered what I was waiting for. Just a little drink, what could it hurt. I could take it. I was the Night Tiger.

Bright light through my window woke me. It was too early for this. I shouldn't have gotten drunk again last night. I knew better and now I had to get up and face another day knowing that I was weaker than I thought. Glancing over at the greasy clock on my old stove, I saw that it was 5 o'clock in the morning. Blinking my eyes rapidly didn't cause the clock to change so I had to accept that it really was way too early to be this bright outside. As drunk as I still was, I immediately knew why. Angel.

Throwing open my window, I leaned out to give her a few choice words that I learned from the fat guy down stairs. She interrupted me with some babble about Primal calling her and then disappearing. The whiskey blurred the finer details but apparently big boy had been kidnapped and was probably gonna be killed at dawn.

Dammit, what does a guy have to do to get some shut eye in this town.

"Okay, I will be right down." I slurred. "I need to sober up with a shower."

"No time," said Angel as an aura of white energy enveloped me.

I was flying again. I really didn't like flying. Jumping across alleyways rooftop to rooftop or dropping off fire escapes was a different matter. I was the one doing the jumping and falling and landing. When flying, I was at the mercy of someone else's superpower. Either way, it was a quick way to travel. We turned to the right. I supposed we weren't taking the tram.

Flying over my turf, I could see the squalor like never before. This was another reason I didn't like to fly. My musing gaze out the window of the tram everyday was more sterile and insulated than this. While flying I could hear the sobbing from open windows and smell the stench of despair that hovered like a dark cloud over my home. My Concrete Jungle.

I know there were predators that I would never catch. Quiet predators that operated in silence and whose prey suffered in isolation. Serial killers and child molesters, spouse abusers and con men, all predators that I could not really fight. Sometimes I wanted to crack those filthy walls open and expose the horrors inside, but I couldn't. I could use my talents against the villains stupid enough to commit their evil in the light of day. As I sped past the decaying tenements, I knew that there were predators within the walls. Predators that I couldn't touch.

"We are getting near the place I think he is being held." said Angel. "Get ready, we are going in hard and fast."

"I'm as ready as I am ever going to be," I replied.

The warehouse was large and most of the windows were spilling yellow light onto the deserted streets. Villains could be seen openly in the alleyways and stairwells surrounding the warehouse. They saw us approach and pointed but took no action against us. It seemed we were expected. This was getting weirder and weirder.

We descended to the front doors and the guards there simply stepped aside and allowed us to enter. Inside was a large room with dozens of thugs lounging around and Primal chained to a chair in the middle, unconscious. Angel and I walked over to Primal and still nobody lifted a finger to stop us. They just watched us and grinned.

41

Angel's blue energy healed Primal and he snapped awake. With a simple motion, Primal broke the chains that held him and stood upright.

"What's going on?" asked Primal.

"I don't know." I replied. "Why aren't they attacking us?"

"Because I haven't told them too, yet!" smiled Angel.

The thugs surrounding us laughed and hooted in derision. Primal looked shocked but I was a step ahead of our good friend Angel. I smiled in return to her and said, "Hello Aurora."

The shock on her face was priceless. I loved when a pretty woman looked surprised. It was so sexy.

"I haven't heard that name in over a decade." she stammered. "How did you know?"

"Shimmer lead me in the right direction." I explained. "I figured out that the three of us had been fighting the actual members of the Shadow Chamber after talking to him."

"Very good." she snarled. "I only figured it out after facing Damia and Brainpain."

"Damia and Brainpain?" asked Primal.

"More recently known as Mediator and Shadow Queen." I supplied. "That means that there are still two members left for us to face. Aurora is Angel, Brainpain is Mediator, Damia is Shadow Queen, Scimitar is Lava Storm, and Cloudburst is Glacier. That leaves only Rock Crusher and Dark Leader to contend with."

"You have it all figured out I see." smiled Angel sarcastically. "Or does he Primal?"

"Well, he had it pretty much figured out." grinned Primal. "Five out of seven isn't bad."

Then it hit me like a ton of bricks. I should have known the second my suspicions about Angel were proven correct. I had felt there was something odd about these two for a while, now I knew who they were. Some detective I am.

"We can put that on his headstone." said Primal, holding his hands up like he was reading a headline. "He had it almost figured out. Great epitaph."

"Figures," I said while shaking my head, "now you see why I don't work well with others."

Angel and Primal shared a glance and began to advance on me. Angel flashed me but I was ready for it and had my head turned and eyes closed. I was not so prepared for Primal's speed as he grabbed my arm and lifted me overhead. I unleashed a flurry of strikes against his wrist but it was like hitting a steel beam. Laughing at my feeble attempts to free myself, he threw me across the room and into a pile of cardboard boxes. Damn, I hated it when they did that.

"You almost had it, Tiger, you were close to the truth," taunted Angel, "but you cannot be blamed for misunderstanding the Chamber. We are not working together, we are competing with each other. Oh, we make alliances like Primal and I or Damia and Brain, but usually we are mostly playing chess with each other using you humans as pawns."

"Now it is becoming clear." I grimaced while trying to stand, "This is just a big game for you but I have two questions."

"Well, I suppose a last request is acceptable." grinned Primal as the assembled punks laughed. "Ask your questions, you can go to the grave with all the answers."

"What about Dark Leader and why me?" I asked.

"The Dark Leader is the only one of us that works alone and hides in the shadows." answered Angel. "After all these centuries, I have only seen him twice."

"As for the other question, it's simple." snarled Primal. "We found it hard to set up our little gambit in your neighborhood with you attacking all the gang's delegates. So, we infiltrated your precinct. I have to admit, Brainpain doing the same was a surprise."

"So, now you know and now you can die." added Angel.

"Well, there is just one small problem with that." spoke a voice from one of the deeper shadows in the room. "Me."

Stepping into the light was a figure very familiar to me. I remembered him taking me as a young man on the mean streets and taming my wild side. I remembered him comforting me when I awoke screaming at the murder of my mother. I remembered him teaching me the way of the tiger. My master.

43

"It has been a long time Aurora and Rock Crusher." serenely smiled the old man. "As usual, your plans lack guile and are full of sound and fury."

Taken aback by the sudden appearance of the old man, Angel and Primal were speechless. I was as well, but that was because I thought my master had died years ago. Seemed like this week was Night Tiger's greatest hits redux.

"I see that my student has broken your precious plan open like a ripe coconut." continued the Master. "One of these centuries, you amateurs will learn some subtlety. Until that day, I will always win our little games."

"Leader." said Angel flatly. "I should have known you would be involved somehow."

"Indeed you should have Aurora," returned the old man, "but you were never very smart, were you? That was always your weakness."

"Come on, Aurora." said Primal. "We lost again."

"Yes, run away Rock." softly chided my master. "That is what you do. You always were a coward."

A peculiar look crossed Primal's face and then his shoulders sagged and he turned to join the flood of gang bangers leaving the building. Angel began to back away with unbridled hate gripping her face.

"This isn't over." she snarled. "I will be back and next time I will be the victor."

"Of course you will, my dear," said the old man condescendingly. "Didn't you say the same thing in England?"

With the villain bravado over with, Angel turned and flew through the open door of the warehouse. My master, the Dark Leader, turned to me. Seeing the look on my face, a wide grin spread across his. Walking to stand before me, he bowed.

"Well, my son, it is good to see you again." smiled the old master. "Do I not get a hug?"

Shock gripping me, I woodenly hugged the man who raised me up to what I was today. I hugged the man who was secretly the man at the center of the Shadow Chamber.

"Master…" I started, "I am confused."

"Do not be, my son." he replied. "Things are not always what they seem. I have been watching you for a while now. I have seen you struggle with your addiction, with your place, with your life. And every time, you ended up doing the right thing. You are nothing but a source of pride for me."

"Thank you, my master." I said. "I am only doing what you have taught me."

"I am sorry that you had to think I died." he said. "It was necessary for your own safety. Those others will stop at nothing to harm me and each other. If I had remained with you, eventually they would have found us. I could not let that happen until you were ready to face them."

"But, you are a villain." I stammered. "You control the Shadow Chamber."

"Yes, I do." he replied softly. "I control them and keep them from spilling their evil game into the streets where thousands would die. I control them by training and helping heroes like you. This was your final test, a lesser man would have walked away a long time ago. You are ready for what you must face. I will not be able to help you with what is to come, but I will send a friend of mine to watch out for you occasionally."

We talked for over an hour. He explained what he had been doing all this time and why he did it. He told me over and over that I was doing the right thing and he was proud. We eventually parted ways with a promise to look each other up again. I headed home with my heart lighter than it had been in years, with my life in perspective like never before. I was slowly beginning to understand my place in the jungle.

The Concrete Jungle.

There was another bottle of whiskey on my table. I didn't know how it got here but it was here now and that was all that matters. The sound it made as I threw it against the wall was liberating. My bed was calling to me and I did not need any self medication to answer it tonight.

I awoke to the sound of an argument next door. At least, I didn't have to deal with it while suffering from a hangover today. A few minutes was all it took to handle all my morning stuff and I was preparing to walk out the door when I noticed an envelope on my table where the bottle was last night. Crossing the room, I picked up the envelope. It was thick and heavy. Opening it showed a sheath of green bills and a small handwritten note that said one thing. I am proud of you.

Walking out of the stairwell, the fat guy started to remind me that today was Thursday and Thursday was rent day. In response, I tossed a couple of bad pictures of Ben Franklin on his desk and flipped him off. He was too busy scrambling for the bills to comment and I was able to escape without hearing his voice again.

Outside, the same old scene was being played out. The flotsam of society was going about it's normal life. Begging and whoring, dealing and scoring, life in the jungle didn't change. I turned to trudge to the tram as I always did. A melodic voice sounded out behind me and I turned to see who was talking to me.

"Good morning, Tiger." smiled Michelle. "It is a pretty day today isn't it?"

Looking around, I suppose she was right. The air was fresh and the sun was warm. I could see some children running and playing in the courtyard of one of the tenements. Their laughter was like bells twinkling in my ear.

"Maybe so, Michelle." I smiled. "How is the new job treating you?"

"It is long and boring but it is less sticky than my last profession." she joked. "That Charley lady is fun to work for though. Thank you again for you help."

"Don't mention it," I said, "you seemed like you were destined for more."

We chatted until we reached the tramway. She was going one way and I was going another. We said our pleasantries and began to go our separate ways.

Turning back to me, she said, "Tiger, would you like to get dinner with me sometime?"

"Do you want me to wear my costume?" I asked. "Ladies love the costume."

"I would prefer if you didn't." her laughter was like a soothing lullaby. "Here is my number at work, call me around lunchtime and we can make some plans."

I agreed and accepted the number. I would definitely be calling her. I got on the tram and, today, I had no desire to spend the time traveling staring out the window morosely. Today might just be a good day after all.

Asphalt Ambush

"Keep your friends close, and your enemies closer."
—Sun-Tzu Chinese general & military strategist

Sunlight wormed it's way into my dreamscape. Groaning in frustration, I rolled over and squeezed my eyes shut. It didn't matter, I was awake now…might as well get up. This early morning shit was for the birds, I say, for da boids. Damn, I'm getting like my grandfather more and more everyday.

I stumbled into the bathroom to see how this morning was treating me. Poorly, I saw. My hair was a mess, short horns sticking up from my pillow's kiss. Dark circles rested under my eyes, won't be needing any eye shadow today. Stubble darkened cheeks completed my morning look. Rubbing my chin, I contemplated a shave but I knew I had a date tonight and 5 o'clock shadow ain't sexy. I'd have to shave after work. A quick shower brought me back to a semblance of life. I pulled on a sweatsuit before grabbing my bag and heading for the door.

I hoped the gym at city hall was empty this morning. I didn't feel like chitchatting today. I slipped down the stairs and out into the street. Funny, nobody paid attention to me when I was not in uniform. I was just a normal guy walking to the tram. I might be getting used to this "Marvin" guy.

Grabbing a paper from the newsstand in the tramway, I settled in for a quiet ride to work. I shoulda known better. This city was never quiet for long.

The automatic door at the end of the car opened with a slight hiss. Three young men strutted into the car. Sneering at the passengers, the punks began to spread out among the seats. Leaning over pretty women and cowering men, the toughs were feeling high on life and some sort of pharmaceutical. I intended to let them have their fun as long as they didn't push it too far. But if you give a teenager an inch, they will take a mile. And these teenagers were no different than any of the others.

One tough, a lanky reed of a kid, grabbed up an icy looking blonde and hooted in pleasure at her shocked expression. Her face was frozen in disbelief for a split second. She overcame her momentary shock and slapped the kid full across the face. Nice shot.

The punk's friends burst into laughter and began taunting him. Slim didn't take kindly to the ribbing and decided he was going to take his frustrations out on Zsa Zsa. He turned back to her after cutting his friends short with a slashing motion from his hand. Bad move.

He grabbed her arm again and yanked her back on her feet with a vicious motion. Twisting her arm with his hand, he drew his other arm back to strike her in the face. Hurling his fist forward, he grinned in anticipation of the contact. The woman flinched in fear as she drew in a gasp of air.

A meaty smack sounded in the tram car like a rifleshot. The woman let out a small peep and fell away from the startled punk. The punk, to his credit, only turned slightly pale as I twisted his extended fist back onto his wrist. Applying pressure, the kid's knees buckled as I pushed harder on my leverage.

"Now, why don't you boys sit down and enjoy the view," I said calmly, "there's no need for anybody to get all worked up this early in the morning."

The tough on his knees, we'll call him Slim Shady, looked up at me with green tinges of nausea in his face. The other two punks started to slide forward to their friend's rescue until they got a good look at my eyes. Something there, call it confidence or even a glint of insanity, gave them enough of a scare that they held their hands up and began to back away.

"How 'bout you, Slim? You walking or are we waltzin'?" I asked with a sarcastic grin.

"Walking, man, I'm walkin'. Just lemme go." hissed the kid through clinched teeth.

"Okay, have it your way." I said as I let him go and sat back down.

The tough took a single look at me and for an instant seemed inclined to push his luck. Common sense took over after that second and the punk slinked off to join his friends. The people in the car had remained silent through the whole ordeal. As the punks exited the automatic door, the passengers exploded with applause.

Red faced, I grinned sheepishly and waved away the applause, "Hey guys, it was nothin'. Any of you coulda done the same thing, just gotta remember that those villains are just punk kids. They only understand the idea that might makes right. Pay attention to your surroundings and, most importantly, stand up for yourselves. They don't want to risk losing to a civilian."

With a nod to the passengers, I opened my paper just as the tram arrived at my stop. Sighing, I folded the paper and stuck it under my arm. Guess I will have to read it after my workout. Strolling out of the tramway, I joined up with a herd of suits on their way to a day of water cooler talk and pencil pushing. I was on my way to slap around cosmic villains and common street trash. You guess which is more fun.

Even at 7am in the morning, City Hall was a busy place. At least two dozen heroes were patrolling or hanging out in the courtyard. I walked through the small groups of spandexes, catching the occasional wave or nod from someone who recognized me without my costume. Reaching the side door, I yanked it open and walked right through Shimmer. I hate it when that happens.

"Sorry Tiger, I knew you would be coming through that door soon," said Shimmer apologetically.

Shaking off the last vestiges of the chill one gets from walking through a ghost, I grinned at him, "Call me Marvin when I am in plainclothes."

"I will try to remember that." nodded the apparition. "The reason I was waiting for you is a feeling I have had recently. I know it is hard for you to understand a ghost "feeling" anything. I am not sure that I understand it either but that doesn't change the fact that I am feeling something."

I was inclined to listen. Shimmer had helped me in the past and I had learned that when the dead speak, it paid to heed them. I held Shimmer's gaze with my own.

"Go on," I said.

"I have had this sense that something wicked this way comes…if you will pardon the pun. Something dark on the horizon, it's something that fills even my cold veins with dread. And for some reason, it involves you," said Shimmer.

"Anything else?" I asked.

"No, just a vague feeling," he replied.

"I'll keep it in mind," I said, "don't hesitate to bring anything else to me. I'll listen."

Nodding, Shimmer turned and floated thorough the adjacent wall. I tell you, it was still a difficult sight to get used too. I turned and headed down the hall towards the gym. Luckily, only a few people were in there working out. Over in the corner was Crowbar, a black dude with superhuman strength. At the moment, he was working the gravity press and I could hear the whine of the machine working in overtime from the doorway. He needed to go easier, he could pull something.

Running on the treadmill was Speedfreak, a tiny woman whose metabolism was 20 times that of a normal person's. She was giving the treadmill a workout, probably surpassing a hundred miles per hour. Her short blonde hair was standing nearly horizontally behind her as she ran. What's the rush?

Walking over to the rubber mat, I stretched out and performed a few simple maneuvers to warm up. Fifteen minutes later, I was hitting the reflex trainers. I'd been feeling a bit slow these last three days. Michelle had keep me running around since our first date. I supposed having a girlfriend can really slow a man down. At least, that was what I've heard.

After half an hour on the reflex trainer, I keyed up a combat simulation and entered the holo-room. As I waited for the room to load and launch the scenario, I allowed myself to relax. The room had finished it's preparations and a yellow light blinked on over the door. Then a blue light...Then a green light...

The room exploded into a chorus of sound and light. When the commotion stopped, the room was gone and in it's place was a burned out street. I was standing right in the middle of a war zone. Rubble laid in piles and litter blew in the rancid breeze. Streetlights were either completely dark or blinked in such a random fashion that the dark seemed more appealing. Slight sounds of movement surrounded me.

From the shadows, punks in leather jackets emerged, lots of punks in leather jackets. Behind me, I could feel several opponents circling me. In front of me, nearly a dozen punks jeered and taunted me. I knew this is a holographic simulation but I could hear their voices and smell their stink. I could see their sneering faces and feel their rage.

One punk stepped forward and pointed at me. A slash of flame streaked from his hand towards me and I spiraled out of it's path. Behind me, I heard a cry of pain as the fireball struck a thug who was trying to sneak up on me. Before I could complete my spin, a figure flashed towards me with swinging fists. I blocked the first two punches but the third slammed into my ribs. I could feel the impact through my armor and a small bit of wind exploded out of me. Recovering from the body blow, I followed through with my slightly bent posture and rammed my forehead into my attacker's face. A crunch of bone greeted my head butt and the punk gurgled out a scream. Massive, tattooed arms wrapped around me and lifted me off my feet in a crushing grip. Already short of breath, purple stars began to dance in front of my eyes as the air was forced out of my lungs. Kicking my heel into Mr. Bear Hug's shin loosened his grip and I slammed my head backwards into the punk's face. Head 2, punk's noses 0.

As the freak dropped me and stumbled backward, I spun around and slammed a kick into his chest. His leg buckled with the impact and he was lifted off his feet. The pile of rubble he landed in made a satisfying noise. As I turned back to the main group of thugs, I noticed one in my peripheral vision drawing a piece. Another punk leapt at me from some trash on my right. I somersaulted away from his sneak attack and grabbed up a crumbling piece of brick. Slamming the jagged edges into his face sprayed blood as I stepped around the fool. Hurling the brick, I was rewarded with the sight of an unconscious punk holding a useless gun. Two of the idiots began to back away as the punk fell, seconds later, they were showing me their backs. Amateurs.

Swiveling my head, I made sure that my back was safe before I turn to the remaining couple of punks. Four of 'em were slowly advancing on me. With a grin, I tried out my new toys. Snapping my wrists, four inch long silver claws appeared at the tips of my fingers. Curved edges captured the uneven light, glinting wickedly. The punks pulled out various weapons. Chains swung and blades cut the air as they advanced.

"Let's dance, boys!" I taunted.

The first one leapt at me with a flashing machete. Swiping the curved blade, I deflected the strike with my claws. Stepping into the punk's space, I swiped at his stomach and was pleased to hear the splatter of organs on the pavement. Gripping his wrist, I spun him into another punk rushing at me with a swinging tire iron. A sickening crunch sounded as the disemboweled punk's face had an unpleasant meeting with the metal bludgeon. Continuing my step, I ended up behind Captain Motor Club. A quick double handed slash put a bleeding "X" on his back and his scream followed me as I sped towards the remaining pair. Gotta watch the splatter, the dry cleaning bill will bankrupt me.

The last two were playing it safe. They circled me in a crouched position, their weapons at the ready. On my left was a dude with a Mohawk expertly wielding a 3 foot length of chain. On my right was the fireball guy lazily swinging a metal bat. Mohawk charged at me with his chain reaching out for my head. Suddenly, he checked his rush and leapt backwards. At the same time, I could feel the heat from Mr. Firebug's silent approach behind me. Snapping back a kick, I caught him off guard and slammed his own bat into his face. Pushing off of him, I leapt past Mohawk with flashing claws. Trust me, it looked cool.

Links of chain fell severed to the pavement with a few grimy fingers thrown in for variety. Mohawk lifted his bleeding hands to his face and fainted with a whimper. Mr. Firebug was still staggering backward with his hand over his face and his bat dropped and forgotten. Rushing him. I leapt at him with my battle claws extended. He reacted suddenly and I realized he had been playing 'possum. Balls of flame erupted around his hands and he blocked my claws with a flash of heat and light. We descended into a violent dance of fire and steel. I slashed him viciously and he burned indiscriminately. Blood sprayed and made our footing slippery, smoke stung our eyes as my costume and skin burned. Savagely, I buried my claws in his gut and, as he screamed, I ripped upward and spilled his life on the ground.

A blinding flash of light and cacophony of noise caused me to stumble slightly. The room returned to it's normal, empty self. My pain disappeared as did the smoking holes in my uniform. The blood and gore dripping from my killing claws vanished as my heartbeat slowed to a more normal pace. Those damn holograms were really convincing.

Sarcastic sounding applause broke me from my revelry. Leaning against the wall beside the doorway was an older man in his early forties bringing his hands together while smiling sarcastically. A receding hairline hovered above graying eyebrows. Watery eyes wryly scrutinized me above a nose red from too much drink too many times. Laugh or frown lines formed creases next to the dude's mouth. A slightly overhanging belly covered most of a rusty hourglass shaped belt buckle. Even so he still carried himself well, as if he used to be someone to watch out for. But not anymore, this guy had really let himself go.

"Nice moves, Tiger!" said the old dude.

I kept my teeth together. I was not gonna be suckered in again. I stared at the dude until he started to get a bit fidgety. Playing with his odd shaped belt buckle, he gave a nervous laugh as he began to speak.

"I know you aren't going to hurt me," he said with a slightly uneasy grin, "I used to be a superhero too. I was a precog, I could see the future. My name was Flashback."

"So, what's the deal fatback?" I snarled.

He winced at my insult. In truth, it wasn't a very nice thing to say but my adrenaline was pumping and that sort of thing was hard for me to control. My mouth was always getting me in trouble. I was trying to quit that.

"Sorry old fella, I'm just a bit worked up right now." Lame apology but better than nothing I supposed.

"No offense taken, I've gotten used to the insults. When you hang up the cape, you become just another regular Joe," he said.

"What can I do for you?" I asked, trying to get to the point.

"There is an ill wind coming and it starts blowing today," said the old man in a shaky voice, "I came out of retirement to try to stop it but I need your help."

"You are the second…person to say something like that to me today," I said, "Why me?"

"I cannot explain it. All my visions have you in them. Some are good and some are bad but they all have one common theme. You," said Flashback matter-of-factly.

"Okay, if you say so. Anything else?" I asked.

"No, that's it. Just be careful out there today." said the old man as he began to walk out the door. "All of you."

Morning briefing was either the most boring, fun time you have ever had or the most fun, boring time you've ever had. Every morning was like a superhero demonstration seminar. Over in one corner would be someone juggling fireballs or someone levitating while in another corner there was hand-to-hand fighting. After a while, it all just became background noise. Today was no different.

Even after Thunderclap had called the meeting to order and begun dispensing assignments, I just couldn't focus. The only thing on my mind was my encounters with Shimmer and Flashback. As usual, I found myself asking why me? And yet again, I had no good answer.

Thunderclap was still droning on about the same old shit. This guy just loved to hear his own voice. I spent a few minutes looking around the room. Near the front sat Electron Storm and Lady Volcano, the two hottest super heroines you would ever see. Their costumes could not make a postage stamp if you sewed them together. It was pretty much unspoken that they were romantically involved with each other. To their left and one row back sat Stink Bomb. He covered the warehouse district and possessed scent glands not unlike a skunk. While not a powerful hero, he was feared nonetheless. Close to him was Neutronix.

He, or more accurately "it", was android and consequently was not affected by Stink Bomb's miasma. Over to my right was Crowbar and Speedfreak. Each senior hero was assigned a junior hero to team with, except me. I was the only hero who did not have a partner. They always got in my way. I just didn't play well with others.

Thunderclap wrapped up his same-old, same-old spiel and I finally tuned back in to his droning. Fixing each of us with his eyes, he drew in a deep breath. As he hit a button on his podium, the lights dimmed and a screen descended behind him.

"This hero's name was Medium," said Thunderclap, a picture of a dark skinned woman appeared behind him, "she was found murdered last night in Port City. She was crucified."

Thunderclap had all of our attentions now. Even I leaned forward to catch all of what he was saying. A dead hero was one thing, it happened all the time. A crucified hero was a totally different story. That was no way for a hero to die. Or anyone, for that matter.

Another picture appeared, this time a light skinned male. "His name was Foreshadow, murdered yesterday evening. He was staked down and burned alive."

"This is Remote View," he said as another picture popped up, "he was one of our clerks. He disappeared three days ago. We investigated and found his house ransacked."

"Three days," I added. "Mediator could have had something to do with it. I could go have a little chat with him. I'll make him talk to me."

Thunderclap was momentarily speechless. I never volunteered anything in the briefings. "Sounds good," he said, "I will send word to the Tower that you have leave to speak with him."

Thunderclap finished up the meeting and everybody headed out to handle their assignments. I walked outside and headed for the tram. I needed to travel past Port City to reach the Tower. My mind wandered as I settled into the almost comfortable bench. The tram left the station and the slow rocking motion caused me to drift off to sleep.

Speedfreak rounded the corner. Moving at a good 90 mph, she sped past cars and people alike. Swerving around a double parked Toyota, she whipped around another corner. She noticed men in orange jackets working on either side of the street. She heard a mechanical whine as she straightened out of the turn. She never saw the steel cable stretched between the buildings. Her last thoughts as her head bounced on the asphalt were that someone should clean up all this blood...

Crowbar was responding to a call on West and 4th when he saw the kids. A dozen of them with water balloons lined the sidewalk. As he looked at them perplexed, they heaved their missiles at him. The balloons popped when they hit him and a funny pungent smell wafted up to his nose, gasoline. He staggered backwards as a group of toughs carrying rocket launchers appeared from the alleyway. One kid flicked a cigarette at the hero's feet and ran as Crowbar burst into a raging fireball. The punks leveled their launchers and fired half a dozen heat seeking missiles into the heart of the inferno. Crowbar was tough, but he wasn't that tough. The explosion shattered windows for blocks and eradicated any trace of the hero.

Stink Bomb saw the guy sneaking around the corner of the warehouse. Signaling to Neutronix, he crept after the thief. He heard scuffling steps from around the corner and stepped around to confront the guy. Bright lights flashed on, blinding Stink Bomb. Men in white chemical suits approached carrying automatic weapons. Stink Bomb unleashed a full spray from his scent glands but the chemical suits protected the men. Their automatic weapons nearly cut the hero in half.

Neutronix saw the lights and heard the shots and flew its fastest to rescue its partner. Swinging around the corner in full combat mode, the android was caught off guard by a simple mesh net. As it tried to rip through the netting, a powerful electromagnetic shock coursed through the mesh. The android's neural net was deactivated instantly.

Electron Storm and Lady Volcano were laying waste to a gang of Hellfires. Storm was manipulating electrical fields and Volcano was hurling lava blasts. Unnoticed, a window on the second story of a nearby building slowly slid open. A slender rifle barrel extended from the open portal. A "chuffing" sound accompanied a small puff of escaping gas as a slender dart rocketed from the barrel. The dart lodged in the upper thigh of Electron Storm who reacted by ripping it out with a cry. Suddenly her legs became wobbly and her powers began firing erratically. Lady Volcano turned to her partner just as lethal bolts of lightning struck her body. Jittering and shaking, Lady Volcano's powers activated and a thirty foot high tower of flame consumed her and her partner.

I awoke from my slumber as the tram was nearing the Tower. Bad public relations for a hero to be caught sleeping on the job but luckily the car was empty. A pleasant chime sounded as the tram pulled up to my stop. Stretching as I stood, I left the tram and walked over to the Tower.

The Tower was a monster of a building. Constructed to house some of the most dangerous beings on the planet, it stretched nearly sixty stories into the sky. Situated nearly a mile from the city, the Tower was protected by some of the best security available. Flights of drone sentries patroled the skies around the vast structure. Multiple fences formed a maze of razor wire looked over by dozens of guard towers. Nearly 500 fully equipped and trained guards tried to keep the lid on the Tower. It wasn't enough, not even close.

The Tower had been originally designed to hold over ten thousand prisoners, including being able to hold over three thousand super powered villains. Due to the changing times and the current upswing of violence, the Tower was operating at nearly three times normal capacity. It was a pressure cooker waiting to explode.

I arrived at the first checkpoint and the guards scanned my ID card. Moments later, a white golf cart rolled up and a driver motioned me into the vehicle. I hopped in and the cart took off with a hum. Watching the multitude of walls and towers even I was impressed with the security.

"Remind me not to end up in here," I mumbled.

"No worries Tiger," replied the guard sarcastically, "I got some soap on a rope for you if you do."

"Thanks, that means a lot to me," I replied with a grin.

I was escorted through the Tower quickly. Thunderclap really had called ahead to get me clearance. I was directed to a small room to await Mediator. The room had gray walls and a single table with two chairs. Overhead, yellow fluorescent lights put an unhealthy glow on the sparse room.

I heard people approaching and I quickly took the seat in front of me. The door across the room opened and two guards led Mediator into the room. A silvery metallic band was on his head and shackles were on his hands and feet. The guards locked him to a metal circlet on the floor as he sat across from me. The guards nodded at me after he was secured and walked out of the room.

"How's the big house treating you, big brain?" I asked.

He grinned at me. "It isn't so bad if you have the right attitude."

"Well, you had better hope you are right because you are going to be in here for a long time," I replied, "50 years wasn't it?"

"I am immortal. 50 years is a twinkle in my eye," replied Mediator unconvincingly.

"Well, if you don't mind hanging around here for the next half a century then be my guest," I said as I slowly rose.

Slight panic appeared in Mediator's eyes. "Hold on, I didn't say I *wanted* to stay here."

"Oh, I must have misunderstood you then," I said as I returned to my chair, "what's that thing on your head, by the way?"

"It is a mental inhibitor. It holds my powers at bay," he answered, "I told them you were immune and it was a waste of our time, but nobody listens to me."

"Do you blame them?" I grinned.

"Not particularly," he beamed in return.

"So, why are all the people who can see the future being killed or kidnapped?" I pressed.

"I wouldn't know," he replied perplexed, "I am…what you would call 'out of the loop' currently."

"C'mon, work with me here," I said.

"Seriously," he said, "I couldn't tell you specifically who or why or how. But I may be able to steer you in the right direction. There is a precedent."

"Okay, lay it on me," I replied.

"Have you ever heard of Morgan LeFay?" he asked.

"Sure, crazy lady who tricked Merlin into getting it on!" I grinned. "Right?"

"Wrong. Morgan Le Fay was a powerful woman who, centuries ago, gathered all the witches and wise women in the land under her rule. She brought them together and used them to attempt to overthrow the King. She used them to murder many men loyal to the King. The King's wizard led his army into the wilds after this woman but she escaped. However, her plan was broken and warped by the passing of history until you have the fairy tale of today," Mediator said.

"Oh…So the right direction is King Arthur's court," I asked, "damn, I hate England."

"No, you buffoon. Morgan LeFay was a real person. A real person who might still be around today. Just because someone is a legend doesn't mean that they didn't exist. We immortals have had many names throughout history. People used to call me Ala'din, among other things," snarled Mediator, "how did you ever defeat me, you simpleton."

"Luck, I suppose," I grinned, "thanks for the help though. I will put a good word in for you if your advice leads to anything."

I pressed the button to end the interview and nothing happened. No guards came to collect Mediator, no footsteps approached the door. I glared at Mediator and he responded with a puzzled, almost fearful look.

"You don't have anything to do with this, do you?" I asked.

"No," he said, "I am as worried as you. When you are in here and something unexpected happens, it is rarely a good thing."

"I understand that feeling," I replied.

I noticed then that the prison was deathly quiet. No yelling, no screaming, nothing but an eerie silence. In this jungle, when the animals go silent that means they are getting ready to pounce. The deeper the silence got, the more it rang in my ear, the more it unnerved me. I could feel the wave rising. Then it crashed.

The noise was earsplitting as if all voices in the facility had been raised in one primal scream. Strain though I might, I couldn't distinguish any single sound. Instead, wave after wave of jumbled, grating, white noise assaulted my senses. I could feel the vibration of the rage. The hate and fear in the air burned my tongue like sticking it to a battery. I couldn't stay here.

One drawback of my intense sensory training was sense overload. Too much noise, too much light, or smells, or tastes, or feelings could cause me to go into minor shock. Right now, I was on the brink. I sank to my knees with my teeth grinding as I tried to hold on to my equilibrium. Mediator shied as far away as his shackles would allow.

"God, what is wrong with you man?" asked Mediator.

"Too much…can't handle the noise…the hate…" I said through a haze of pain.

"If you will help me, then I can help you," said the villain.

I don't make deals with villains, I stop them and lock them up. At the moment, however, I might not have had much of a choice. Straining to raise my head, I locked eyes with him. Something in there told me to take my chances with his offer. I nodded.

"Take this thing off my head," he said as he leaned towards me.

The room was covered in a red haze but I lifted my arm towards him. He reached out and grabbed my wrist. Together, we were able to get my hand on the headband. Removing it was simple, I held on to it while he let go of my arm. Gravity did the rest. The second that the strip of metal was torn from his brow, he squinted his eyes and I began to feel instant relief. Within moments, my head was clear and I was able to stand. Taking a step, I leaned against the table as I regained my strength.

"What did you do?" I asked.

"I shut down your sensory centers for about an hour, which is about the only thing I can with a mind as strong as yours. That means we have about 55 minutes before they come back and you collapse again," he replied, "don't you think that you should figure out a way to get me free of these?"

He shook his manacled hands at me. My strength had returned enough for me to step over and grab the chain holding his hands. Popping my claws, I slashed through the links in one swipe. As the metal clattered to the floor, Mediator stared at my claws.

"Those are new," he said.

"Be proud. You are the first crook to see them," I grinned.

"I resent that. I am more than a mere crook, I am an evil genius," he replied.

I laughed, I couldn't help myself. Mediator was fun to talk too. Shaking my head at his humor, I began to slide to the doorway. His voice a hiss, Mediator called out to me to stop.

"Wait. There are people out there," he warned, "and the only thing on their minds is ambushing you and capturing me."

"Who?" I asked as I crouched near the door.

"They are nobodies. Common street trash hired to do a job," he answered, "and, no, they don't know who hired them. That was the first thing I checked…"

Nodding, I glance suggestively at the door and he dipped his head in agreement. Leaping at the door, I grabbed the knob and jerked the door open. The second that the door began to move, I picked my feet up and rode it as it swung.

Gunfire filled the air that I had just occupied for a few seconds before the assassins could get their reflexes under control. They must have acquired some firearms from the guards. The silence was thick as the moments slipped past. A slight scuffing noise and the tinkle of a shell casing betrayed the men moving outside. We both knew that each other was there. So, let's give 'em a surprise.

I leapt into the open doorway, in front of me were two men dressed in black jumpsuits. Both held automatic weapons at the ready. Starting slightly at my sudden appearance, the men had no chance as I stepped between them and slashed through their abdominal wall. I continued my forward motion and both men spun towards me while firing their weapons.

They stitched themselves with bullets as I moved towards two men to my right. They struggled to get their weapons aimed at me as I erratically swerved in front of them. Each time that their weapons were almost trained on me, I was suddenly moving the opposite direction. And each time those weapons lost me, I moved a step closer to the gunmen. Before they knew it, I was upon them and slashed through their firing arms. Screaming in agony, they fell backwards holding their bleeding extremities. A sounded step behind me.

A powerful blow smashed into my back. Stumbling forward, my head impacted with the wall in front of me. Rebounding off, I took a major punch in the kidneys. Trying to hold my back and my head at the same time as I fall is not an easy thing to do. Somehow I accomplished it.

"On your feet," snarled a voice I almost recognized, "it's not going to be that simple."

Slowly and painfully, I began to rise. As I turned to face my attacker, I could feel my legs trembling. Sometimes, when a person gets hit in the kidneys hard enough, they lose the muscle control in their legs. This was one of those times. I was what the old fellas called "weak in the knees". Leaning against the wall to support myself, I was able to turn and face my attacker.

A shock of dark hair was plastered above a youthful face. His red, irritated eyes glared at me as the man grinned savagely at my pain. His fingers had hooked into claws as the shadows deepened in the hallway. Déjà vu.

"Yeah, it's me," said Darkfall, "did you think we were finished? We've only just begun."

"Man, you're pushing your luck, kid," I mumbled as I tried to clear my head, "I was going easy on you to begin with."

"I nearly lost my sight because of you!" he snarled as he leapt at me.

I had lots of choices. I could leap aside, or I could snap a kick at him to keep him back, or I could take his charge and try to wrestle with him. After microseconds of deliberation between my demanding head and my wobbly legs, I decided the best course of action was to simply drop to the floor and crawl away. Good plan.

Darkfall smashed face first into the wall as I fell to the floor. As I tried to crawl away, he staggered towards me. Slashing feebly at his leg, I opened up four minor wounds on his right calf. He sucked air through clenched teeth as the blood began to flow. I kept crawling.

Stomping footsteps combined with sliding footsteps told me that he was nearly upon me. Rolling onto my back I kicked out blindly, connecting with his left knee. With both legs injured, he simply fell on top of me. Savagely, we began to tear into each other. I couldn't tell you how many times he hit me or I cut him. It seemed like we were locked into a whirlwind of pain for an eternity when he triumphantly grabbed my neck with both hands and began to squeeze. Panicking, I thrashed violently and burned through my scant oxygen even quicker. Flashing lights began to "pop" before my eyes…a long, dark tunnel appeared on the corners of my vision…my chest burned…I could hear myself making strange, pained "hiccupping" noises from a long distance away…the world began to strobe…WHAM!

I felt a huge impact, followed by the sound of a body hitting the floor next to me. I drew in a ragged breath that screamed in my tortured throat. Straining, I opened my eyes and saw Mediator standing over me holding a rifle. Looking beside me, I saw Darkfall on the floor.

"He is one tough cookie, that's for sure," He said as he looked at the fallen villain and then me, "you're not so bad either."

Taking his outstretched hand, I let him pull me to my feet. Staggering in place, I put a hand on the wall next to me to steady myself. Taking stock, I was weak and battered and nearly useless. Mediator placed his hand under my arm and started to help me walk.

"Go on," I said as I tried to resist him, "I'll just slow you down. You helped me, I helped you. We're even."

"Yeah, we are," he replied, "so you will just have to owe me one."

Half carrying, half dragging, he was able to get me to the end of the hall. He leaned me against the wall and then he peeked through the door's porthole. I could see him turn pale before my eyes. That was usually not a good sign.

"What is it?" I asked through a haze.

"You don't want to know," he replied, "we can make it. I can keep us hidden in the minds of those around us. But…"

"But what?" I demanded.

"Just try to control yourself when you see. If you react, we are both dead men," he said as he scooped me up and pushed the door open.

Waking the Devil

"Tears, such as angels weep, burst forth."
—John Milton, Paradise Lost

We stepped onto a balcony overlooking hell. Chaos reigned as psychotic killers with super powers unleashed death upon each other. Flames danced and lightning scattered as blood fell in fat drops. The floor of the room was a sea of offal that reached nearly ankle deep. The guards had been taken captive and were suspended in the middle of the large room on makeshift crucifixes. Presiding over the circle of sacrificed men was a tall, slender maniac glowing with an unearthly light. He moved about the circle of crucifixes chanting and weaving strands of energy in an indiscernible pattern.

"Jesus…What the hell is that Mediator?" I stammered.

"Hell is exactly what that is and Jesus can't help," he replied as we hurried to the staircase, "some fool let the Summoner out of his cell. He is calling forth the Demonlord Agzamoth."

"We…we have to stop him," I said through clenched teeth.

"It's too late. There's nothing we can do," said Mediator while dragging me to the top step.

As he said it, a strange silence descended upon the room. The dozens of villains killing each other stopped and turned towards the now glowing circle. Inside the circle, a shape coalesced from glowing shadow to horrible flesh. Agzamoth was in this world. Striking forward with unnatural speed, the demon ripped the Summoner's head from his shoulders and swallowed it whole. Then the monster stood and faced the room.

Towering nearly twenty feet tall, the demonlord was a being of gut wrenching terror. Mottled red and black skin was covered in leathery scales. A perfect physique was marred by a stunted and feral posture. Massive arms ended in long black claws that glittered in the disappearing glow. Goat-like legs with cloven hooves stomped impatiently while a long leathery tail curled and twitched. Large batwings unfurled and stretched wide. A face not unlike that of a human's adorned the creature. The main differences were the long chin and the two large black horns that curled from it's forehead. Solid black eyes swept the room, pausing and narrowing for a moment when they neared us. Long fangs appeared as the creature opened it's mouth and bellowed chillingly evil laughter.

Mediator began to drag me down the staircase as the demon stalked into the stunned villains. Snatching one up, Agzamoth effortlessly tore him in half. Holding the halves above his head, the demon drank deeply of the villain's lifeblood. The grotesque tableau shocked the villains into action and they unleashed amazing amounts of power into the beast. Red flesh burned and black blood sizzled. Bones were snapped and organs were crushed. The demonlord howled in agony and retaliated by sweeping his claws into a mass of villains, ripping them in half with a single swipe. Turning like a massive wolf held at bay by a pack of dogs, the demon killed with every step. And with every death, the monster grew in power.

Reaching the bottom of the staircase, Mediator half guided, half dragged me to a large hole in the wall under the staircase. Tearing my eyes from the carnage inside, I viewed the carnage outside. Hundreds of villains had still been inside the prison, thousands had already escaped. In doing so, they had laid waste to the fences and guard posts. Nearby, the tram station burned and the rails were destroyed. The fields between the prison and the city were thick with escaping villains.

"Where are the heroes?" I gasped.

"I would bet they are all dead or otherwise incapable of coming," replied Mediator as he helped me limp through the broken fences, "when le Fay attempted to overthrow Uther and his knights, she assassinated as many as she could before making her move. I would bet she did the same thing this time."

Reaching the last fence, Mediator pointed towards a nearby copse of trees. "I'm going to put you there. You will regain your senses in about 15 minutes. I will stay with you until then, afterwards, you're on your on."

"Thanks," I said, "I won't forget this."

"You will have need of me soon," he replied, "when the time is right, I will be there."

I nodded. We were quiet as we reached the trees. Amazingly, none of the inmates were hanging out in there and I was able to get a bit of wind back before my senses came flooding back to me. The shock nearly drove me to my knees but I was able to shake it off and remain standing. Mediator looked me over, nodded once, and disappeared from sight. He hadn't disappeared, I realized, he had made me think I couldn't see him.

I rested for a few more minutes and began my long trek back into town. By then, the fields were empty. As I left the trees and entered the field, I looked back at the prison. Smoke curled from every available orifice. The grounds were in ruins. Bodies littered the landscape. A huge gaping hole lay in the wall of the building. Shadows moved inside and I was sure I could feel hateful eyes resting on me. Shivering, I looked away and set off for the city.

Port City lay in ruins. The waters of the bay burned with blue flames as oil from a destroyed tanker covered the surface. Buildings had that shelled out look that reminded me of old movies about World War 2. Trash littered the streets and people were both scarce and scared. Flames danced in a few buildings and everywhere was chaos and destruction. Passing a thrift shop with broken windows, I grabbed a long brown coat from a rack near the entrance. Throwing the coat on over my costume, I slowly trudged towards the nearest Law Enforcement Station. A cold rain began to fall.

East Port Station was a squat bunker-like building made of concrete and steel. A few functioning police drones still patrolled the airspace above the station. Intermittently, an energy beam would flash from one of the drones to strike the horde attacking the station. At least fifty villains were amassed outside as a handful of heroes tried to defend against them. The villains were unleashing their might upon the defenders but the heroes were holding their own for the moment. Let's end this square dance.

Running toward the slimmest section of villains, I began to lay into them with my claws extended. I held back as much as possible and didn't unleash any killing blows. I slashed the first two across their backs. They fell to the ground screaming and contorting their bodies trying to grab hold of the pain. One guy turned and I kicked him full in the face. He flew backwards, taking three others to the ground. Spinning on my heel, I punched another villain in the armpit. Grabbing another, I pulled his head down as I brought my knee up and flipped him head over heels with the impact. The three that had been knocked off their feet were struggling to get up as another thug leapt over them and charged at me. Meeting his charge with a sidestep, I grabbed his arm and kicked out. Sweeping him off his feet, I twisted and hurled him into another two punks. Suddenly, I could see daylight.

Bounding a few steps, I leapt into the air and split kicked the two closest villains as they began to turn to the commotion. Both went down as I landed and ran towards the besieged heroes. Jogging to a stop, I nodded at the five spandexes huddled in the Station's courtyard.

"Who's in charge?" I demanded.

"You are," said a short man, "our captain's dead and our lieutenant has been missing for two days."

"Okay," I said, taking control, "the punks outside are a buncha wimps. Are any of you heavy hitters?"

"I am," said a slender man in a blue and red suit, "but I burn out quickly."

"No problem. They will break and run if we look like we are winning," I replied, "follow me."

Leading the group of heroes towards the rabble, I began to jog. The heroes picked up their pace to keep up with me. The hero in blue and red loosed a loud battle cry while a red hair woman beside him summoned lightning around her hands. As we neared the throng of villains, the punks began to edge away. As I jump kicked the first one I got near, they began to break. As the blue and red dude slammed his hands into the pavement and knocked half a dozen villains off their feet with a rolling wave of concrete, they began to run. As the redhead unleashed a storm of lightning and thunder, it was a rout. We broke off chase and watched the punks scatter.

"Red, you are on sentry duty. Call us if those guys come back," I said as I pointed at the redhead. "the rest of you, come with me."

I walked into the Station without checking to see if anyone followed. Inside, the Station was a mess. It looked like someone pulled the pin on a garbage grenade and tossed it into the room. Walking around the booking desk, I grabbed one of the overturned chairs and sat down.

"Grab a seat, heroes," I said as I swept my hand towards some overturned chairs, "what's your names and powers?"

"I'm Mr. Excellent," said the blue and red suited hero, "I break things but the harder I fight the quicker I get worn out."

"I'm Interface," said a slightly chubby hero in a suit festooned with pouches, "I possess the ability to operate any machine. I'm more of a clerk than a field agent."

"Myrmidon is my name," said an older woman, "my psychic abilities allow me to control others. Though I am limited in the number that I can control at any given time."

"Lady Artemis here and I am an archer," said a slender woman in a tech suit as she held up a fancy compound bow, "and the girl outside is Storm Front. She can call up thunderstorms."

"Not bad," I said, "my name is Night Tiger."

"We know. You are a bit of a legend," said Excellent.

Shrugging, I said, "Maybe so, has there been any word from City Hall?"

"There were reports of a large mob of villains marching on City Hall. We mobilized to go to the rescue and ran into our own mob," said Interface, "we captured a few before they murdered Nova Burst, our captain. We had all just gotten here, we don't know where the morning shift is."

"They are probably dead," I said.

"What happened?" asked Artemis, "Where did they all come from?"

"Prison break," I said simply.

"How many escaped?" asked Myrmidon.

"Thousands," I answered.

The heroes were speechless for a few minutes as they pondered the effect that thousands of hardened supervillains would have on the city. Needless to say, it wasn't going to be a good effect. Breaking the quiet, I cleared my throat and they all turned to look at me.

"Here is the plan," I said, "we release the prisoners in the holding cell. We cannot afford to keep people here to take care of them. Interface, you are to get on the 'net and track down as many heroes as you can. I mean, second stringers, retired heroes, wannabes, dropouts. Everybody. Sound a call to arms."

"Will do," he replied.

"Excellent, you and Myrmidon head outside and help Storm Front with sentry duty. Try to get those sentries back online, the couple we have right now will not stop another concentrated attack," I ordered, "Artemis, you come with me…We are letting those prisoners go."

They all hopped to their tasks. Having someone give orders in a time of crisis was a godsend for morale, it didn't matter if the orders make sense or not. And for that I am glad. Interface hurried over to a computer station and was busy typing away like a madman. Mr. Excellent and Myrmidon walked outside together as Artemis and I headed towards the holding tanks.

The atmosphere in the holding tank was so tense it was almost suffocating. The cells were full of villains who stared at us reproachfully. Stepping up to the first door, I nodded at Artemis who nocked an arrow in her bow. I opened the door.

"Get out of there, punk!" I said to the bewildered villain.

Looking at me with apprehension, the kid slid out of the cell slowly. Every step he took was covered by Lady Artemis's bow. The kid backed away from us, and wild-eyed, he ran from the room. I turned to next cell and repeated the action. After a few minutes, the cells were clear and all of the bad guys had left peacefully.

"Why did we just do that, may I ask?" said Artemis.

"I told you, there is no way we can spare the manpower to keep them here. And I wouldn't leave them here alone," I said.

"Why not?' she asked.

"Because none of us may live through the next twenty four hours and villain or not, I will not let them starve to death in a cage," I explained.

"Well, when you put it that way," said the archer with a grin, "I suppose I have to agree!"

We headed back into the main room just as Interface was finishing up work on a small machine. His computer was buzzing and humming and generally making a racket. Hurrying over to the machine, he pressed a button and a sleeve extended from the hard drive. Taking a tiny disk from the sleeve, Interface turned and placed it in the funny little machine he was working on. Grabbing a screwdriver, Interface completed the machine and screwed it's casing closed.

"Whatcha got there?" I asked.

"It's an amusing little toy. It's calibrated with the information on the heroes who did not answer the call to arms. The information is cross referenced with all knowledge about the heroes in question and can extrapolate where they may be to a fair degree of accuracy," explained Interface, "it's for you."

"Thanks," I said as I accepted the small device.

"Don't mention it," said Interface, "just glad to do my part."

"There is another thing you can do," I said, "I need someone to coordinate the heroes and assemble them into strike forces. Want the job?"

"Does it have good benefits?" he asked with a grin.

"The best!" I replied.

"Then I am your man," said Interface.

By then, the first groups of heroes were assembling at the Station. Currently, according to some of them, we were the only heroes that had defended their Station. As more heroes began to assemble and Interface began to put them in proper squads, I checked out the names on my list.

The first name was Junkyard. The funniest thing was that I knew exactly where to find him. He was in the same place he always was. Grabbing a comm unit from Interface, I set off to round up some reluctant heroes.

The Eastside Junkyard took up over ten city blocks. Inside the tall concrete walls, mountains of scrap metal and broken toys reached for the sky. Sitting in front of a ramshackle building was a squat man. His hat was pulled down, shading his eyes from the afternoon sun. He gave no signal that he heard my silent approach. Until he spoke to me.

"Don't care," he said gruffly.

"You haven't heard what is happening, Jeff," I said.

At the mention of his name, he looked up and grinned at me. "Well, I'll be damned. They sent you? Talk about scraping the bottom of the barrel."

"I volunteered. I didn't think any of the others could handle the stench!" I grinned.

"It's been a long time, man," he said as he grinned and hugged me, "too long."

"It's good to see you too, Jeff," I said, "how have you been?"

"Not bad. The junkyard business is quiet and makes steady money. At least in this city, it does," he said.

"So, are you bored with it yet?" I chided, "Maybe enough to put your suit back on."

"That ship has sailed, my friend. You know that. You were there when they railroaded me into this life as a civilian. They were the ones who wanted me to be a junkman instead of a hero," he shook his head, "No, I think the suit stays where it belongs...in a display case."

"Dammit, Jeff. That was a long time ago. We need you. There was a prison break," I pleaded.

"Damn, how many escaped?" he asked.

"All of them," I answered, "well, the ones that didn't get killed by that demon lord, that is."

The man who refused to be a hero anymore sat back against the wall of his broken down house in the middle of a junkyard and contemplated what I had just said. He shook his head finally. "Nice try man. But that is too farfetched even for you."

"It's true. I was there," I said matter-of-factly.

For a minute, he sat there and stared at me. Then he turned his head and began to look around the junkyard. He looked back and me and nodded. His eyes were narrowed.

"Okay, I'm in. Gimme a minute to get my suit and I will meet you wherever you tell me," he said, "Junkyard is back in the game."

"And it's about time, too," I said, "I have a few other heroes to contact. Meet me at the Patriot tramline near City Hall in one hour. Be careful."

He nodded at me and walked into his house. I stared at his back for a minute and pulled out my little data screen. The next hero was called Jinx and I had heard of her already. Hell, most of the people in this city had heard of her. When you saw Jinx, it was best for you if you turned around and went the other way. This was gonna be fun.

I hurried over to the Gateway Mall. It was packed. Even with a major threat to the city in the form of a jailbreak, commerce goes on. Entering the mall, I beelined for one of those map kiosk thingies. I quickly found the store I was looking for under "stores that a guy would never go in…unless they are gay…And I mean REALLY gay". Definitely not my kind of store.

Anyway, entering the store I realized that I will never find her. The store is filled with a bevy of blonde bubbleheads buying baubles…I love alliteration. Jinx was a blonde beauty as well, so I decided right then and there that a direct approach was the best. Raising my hands, I bellowed out the word "JINX!"

All of the girls turned and look at me like I was crazy…And maybe I was…but one in particular squinted her eyes at me with an angry look. Jinx. She was an extremely attractive blonde girl. Well endowed with an angel's face and a devil's temperament, she was going to make a lot of men unhappy in her life. She put her purchases down and walked out of the store while glaring at me. I grinned sheepishly at the other girls in the store before I gave chase.

"Hold up, Jinx," I said as I reached for her arm.

"Don't touch me!" she snarled as she yanked her arm away from my reach.

"Hold up," I repeated.

She stopped and slowly turned around with fire in her eyes. This was one girl who did not take kindly to anyone standing in her way.

"What?" she drew out the word.

"There has been a prison break. The city has need of you," I explained, "please, Jinx. I understand about what happened but times have changed and this is your chance. Most people don't get another chance."

"I don't want a chance," she said with an angry voice, "I just want to be left alone. I wanted to be a hero once but the people of this city didn't want me. So, screw them."

She turned and walked away. I hurried to match her stride and quickly caught up with her. "Stop it, Jinx. People are going to die, people have already died. I watched it happen. We need you, insurance lawyers or not. We need you Jinx."

"I don't care," she said.

"Do you remember Speedfreak?" I asked.

"Of course I do. We were in the same graduating class at the Academy. Talk about hyper, she never shuts up!." grinned Jinx.

"She's dead," I said, "I found out earlier that she had been decapitated. Decapitated, Jinx."

I turned and walked away from her. "If you ever decide to be who you really are, then meet me at the Patriot Line in 45 minutes. If not, then I heard there is a sale at Claires. Lottsa good bargains."

I could feel her eyes on my back as I stalked away. I did not have time to beg every hero with an inferiority complex into helping save lives. Either they went along or they didn't. And truth be told, it probably wouldn't matter if every hero in the city answered the call. It probably still wouldn't be enough.

There were three names left. I checked the first one and saw it was a precog, as was the second. I already knew why they didn't answer. Then I saw the name of the final hero I was supposed to find. The last name was Flotsam and if I thought I dreaded talking to Junkyard and Jinx, then Flotsam was ten times worse.

The last time I had entered the sewers of the city was when I was chasing some thieves that used plumbing to access stores. It had smelled bad then and it smelled worse now. I hurried down a large sewer pipe but I was running out of time. If I didn't find her soon, I was going to have to write her off and head for the tram. The small device that Interface had put together for me beeped twice. Checking it, I turned left and ran smack into a group of vagabonds. Swarming me, they had me restrained in a heartbeat and began carrying me deeper into the maze of pipes.

A few minutes later I was carried into a large cavern like room with a river of sewage running through it. Hundreds of dirty ragamuffins filled the room. The group that had me carried me before an upraised platform and dumped me on the dirty floor. One guy began beating two trashcan lids together rhythmically. After a few minutes the flow of the sewage increased alarmingly. Suddenly a wave of sewer water flowed down the center of the room. Riding the crest of the water was a filthy looking person. Rags covered it concealing features as effectively as a burkha. The water crested to a stop beside me and the person walked across the suddenly placid surface. Stopping in front of me, the person spoke.

"Well, look what cat we drugged in, boys," said Flotsam, "it's the infamous Night Tiger."

"Hello Flotsam. Long time, no smell," I said.

"Always the kidder, eh Tiger?" she said as she knelt down to my level. "Well, I would watch your tongue in here. My boys don't take kindly to insults, friends or no friends."

"No offense intended then. The last thing I need right now is more trouble, especially from your Wild Boys," I said disarmingly.

"Cut to the chase. I know my emergency beacon went off half an hour ago. Now, you come sniffing around down here. Only something really big would bring you down to our level. What is it?" demanded Flotsam.

"Listen, there was a prison break. If I can find you then so can the bad guys. And when they are done with us, they will be coming for you," I explained, "by helping us, you are helping yourselves. And that is what you have always been about Sam...helping yourself."

"Oooh, low blow, Tiger. Low blow," smiled Flotsam, "well, surface problems are for surface dwellers. Here in the Underworld, we have our own problems. If you surface dwellers had helped us before, we would help you now. But you didn't."

She turned and walked away from me. "Thanks for stopping by. The next time you show up down here, we will kill you."

"Fair enough, Sam. But turn your back on us at your own risk, that just means that we might not be there for you when you do really needs us," I replied as the Wild Boys drug me off, "in fact, I can guarantee that without your help we will fall. If we fall, then eventually so do you.

Flotsam stopped and held up her hand. The Wild Boys holding me froze and waited for her signal. Nodding to them, she said. "So be it." and turned away.

"So be it," I repeated as they carried me away, "So be it."

I was running late. I had about 5 minutes to go ten minutes worth of distance. I wasn't going to make it. Cranking up my speed, I felt as if my lungs would burst as I hurtled headlong to my destination. Spots burst in front of my eyes as I struggled for breath each pounding step I took. Rounding the corner near the tram, I saw flames around the station and a small group of villains dancing around like madmen at the tram's base.

In a nearby alley, I could see the silhouette of a man in a large uneven set of armor. Hurrying over, I dodged into the alleyway. Rapping Junkyard on his armor to get his attention, I nodded to the tram.

"Like that when you got here?" I asked.

"Yep, but I just got here," he answered, "I think I am the first."

"You may be the only, not just the first," I grinned sarcastically, "You are the only one I was sure I would get."

"Did you count on me?" said a voice behind me.

I spun in time to see a man stroll up in a ludicrous red and gold costume from the early 80s. Absolutely ugly, the costume had the most garish color scheme I had ever seen with flaring boots and a sash. Let me repeat that, a sash!

"No, and I still not counting you," I replied, "how did you find us, Flashback?"

"I can see the future. Remember?" he answered, "I know my destiny as well as I know my own name."

"So, what's the plan then?" asked Junkyard, "The same old plan you usually have? Go punch the bad guy?"

"Yep, sounds good to me," I grinned as I started to stand.

"Wait," said Flashback, "we have someone else coming, soon."

"I never understood why you fortune tellers have to be so cryptic all the time. Why not just tell me who is coming instead of making me wonder?" I chided.

"I cannot, the probabilities are not set in stone. There are several people who could show up but only one will," answered Flashback, "the sooner to arrival, the sooner I will know with a certainty who it is."

"I suppose that will have to do." said Junkyard.

A few minutes passed as the punks surrounding the tram increased the fury in which they were celebrating the destruction they caused. Junkyard was fidgety, once back in his armor he couldn't wait to try it out again. I was merely bored while Flashback sat on a wooden box serenely. Suddenly he looked up.

"Oh no," he said.

"Oh no? Oh no what?" I asked. "What?"

"Hold onto your hats," said Flashback.

I was about to demand to know what he meant when I heard a funny whistling noise. I couldn't place it but when I looked at Junkyard, he was looking up in a stupor. Coming around the bend was the tram and it was flying. On the roof of the front car was a beautiful blonde girl in an eye-popping costume. As the tram approached the blazing station, the girl leapt off into space to her sure doom. As she plummeted, I noticed a wire sticking across her path. She hit the wire at full speed and it ripped from its anchor. The line swung down from her weight and she gently alighted on the asphalt as the tram rocketed into the station. The explosion was fantastic.

When the dust settled, the tram station was obliterated and the villains surrounding it were now smoldering corpses. The girl looked at her handiwork and shrugged. Stepping up to her, my eyes begged a question.

"What?" she said slowly.

"Did you have to kill them Jinx?" I asked carefully, "And why did the tram go up like that?"

"I didn't mean to kill them but my unpredictability power is just that, unpredictable," she said, "as for the tram, as amazing as it sounds, I think I was riding one that carried explosives. You know how things tend to blow up when I am around. Why do you think they made me take off the cape?"

"Well, you certainly make a big entrance, Jinx," said Junkyard, his eyes wide at her beauty, "my name is Junkyard."

"It fits," said Jinx sarcastically.

"Enough with the banter. We have a job to do," I said, "unless you have another prediction of someone else coming."

"No, the other players are about their own business," answered Flashback, "now, we need to see to ours."

City Hall was about two blocks from the tram station. Even from that far away, we could hear the sounds of a major battle in progress. Hurrying towards the center of the confusion, we rounded a corner and got our first glimpse of City Hall. At one time, it was the most impressive building in the city. Now it was besieged by a thousand villains. The police drones sent down a steady stream of energy but did little to stop the onrushing hoards. A few stalwart heroes defended the entrances to the building. In front of us were a hundred or more villains throwing fireballs, calling down lightning, and summoning dark energies. Basically, they were throwing down with some super powers. Let's see how they like similar treatment.

Catching Junkyard's eye, I nodded my head in the direction of the nearest bad guys. He grinned and charged straight at them, his armor clanking with each step. A few turned at his approach but to no avail. He hit the wall of thugs and flattened dozens of them. Nearly all of them turned at the sound of impact and got their first look at my new claws. Slashing wildly, I cut a path through the punks. I was careful to not kill any of them but there were a bunch of them who would be taking meals out of straws for a few weeks. Jinx stood her ground as a few thugs charged at her. As they got near, one tripped over his own feet and stumbled into another. The two went down in a bone crunching pile as the third leapt over them. As he landed, his feet slid on a piece of newspaper and as he stumbled forward, Jinx punched him in the eye. The punk was unconscious before his head hit the pavement. I noticed Flashback hanging back and suddenly a punk rose up behind him with a knife. I turned to shout out a warning as Flashback sidestepped the punk's thrust and punched him in the gut. The punk doubled over and Flashback caught him with a solid right hook. They are okay. Watch your own back.

Sage advice, I thought as I was tackled from behind. The kid who hit me drove me into the ground. Rolling over, I struggled to free myself from his grasp. Punching him hard in the side broke a couple of his ribs and forced him to protect himself. A follow up punch cracked his jaw and knocked him out. Crawling from under him, I momentarily found myself in a relative island of calm.

Looking around, I saw Junkyard knocking two or three villains flat with each swing of armored fists. Jinx was standing calmly around a growing pile of stumbling and bumbling villains. None of them were getting close to her without being affected by her unpredictability and none were able to draw a bead on her from a distance. Flashback was simply jogging around the battlefield, calmly, slowly, infuriatingly dodging anyone who got near him. His precognitive ability enabling him to dodge every attack before it was even conceived. I glanced at the larger group of villains who were just now beginning to notice the four of us. I knew right then. We were not going to make it.

Against a hundred punks of this caliber, we stood a decent chance. Against ten times that number we were toast. Slowly, the massive army of supervillains turned and began to advance on us. The sheer weight of numbers were overwhelming. I ended up fighting a dozen men at once while a half dozen others launched volleys of energy at me. Junkyard got buried under a wall of thugs, the pile shaking as he tried to stand. Jinx's field got overloaded by too many people entering it and winked off. She found herself surrounded by a ring of very angry thugs. Flashback reached the point where he could find no avenue of escape and got tripped up by a stumbling villain.

Just as I was going down under a mass of enemies, the communication unit I had picked up garbled something. In the pile of bodies I couldn't understand it, the only thing on my mind was that I was about to die. Suddenly, some dynamic on the battle field changed. While I still found myself fighting for my life, many of the punks on top of me were scrambling away. Biting an arm that was trying to cut off my air supply by crushing my neck, I noticed that I was surrounded by fewer assailants.

Pushing the fool I had just bitten away, I crawled out of the pile of unconscious and injured villains. In the sky were angels. Golden beings calling down the fury of justice. On the battle field fought avatars of destruction.

The cavalry had arrived. Nearly one hundred heroes struck the disorganized villains in waves of furious intensity. Powers unleashed and mixed to destructive affect. Bodies flew as villains were struck senseless from the sheer power laid down. But the heroes were not unscathed. Some villains gave as well as they got and dozens of the good guys fell. It seemed the battle was tipping in favor of the much larger force of thugs when a ragged battlecry sounded. What the hell?

A wave of water crashed into the southern flank of the mob. Behind the massive wave ran an army of screaming vagabonds with a woman at the front riding a stallion of pure water. Hundreds of pissed off sewer dwellers led by a hero able to manipulate water with a thought slammed into the mob of villains. Flotsam and the Wild Boys were here.

The spectacular arrival of the army of bums was enough to break the fading morale of the villains. They ran from battle as if the devil himself chased them. And judging from what I had seen at the Tower, he might have been. The heroes were, for the most part, too tired to give chase. When the villains ran, most of the heroes still standing collapsed to their knees in exhaustion.

Looking around, I saw Junkyard slowly standing in the middle of a large pile of groaning thugs. His left shoulder had taken a lot of damage and his arm hung limply at his side. Over to his right, Jinx stumbled toward me cradling her right arm. He skimpy outfit was torn in quite a few places and was bordering on indecent. Blood flowed freely from a few wounds on her torso but she seemed to be alright. Swiveling my head, I saw a pile of villains a few yards behind me. Stepping over to it, I began to push the thugs to the side. Junkyard stumbled over and helped me move the bodies faster. At the bottom of the pile lay the broken and twisted body of Flashback. He had borne the brunt of damage as the wave of villains had crashed upon us. The sheer weight had crushed the life out of him and two of the thugs.

Rolling him over onto his back, I was struck by the look on his face. Serene, almost happy, his face was at peace. Flotsam walked into my field of vision as I stared down at the fallen hero. Stepping next to me, she caught my eye and then stared down at Flashback.

"Do you know why he retired?" asked Flotsam

"No, he never said why," I answered.

"He foresaw his own death, he knew that he would die if he put that uniform back on," she said, "and he still did. I remember that he got tormented by the other heroes for hanging up his cape because he was scared to die. I guess he proved that he wasn't that scared after all."

"He fought well," I said simply, "he was a brave man."

"I didn't know him well, but he impressed me," said Junkyard, "I thought he was going to be the first to fall and he ended up lasting longer than all of us."

"At the beginning of the battle, he ran past me and whispered that I shouldn't worry," said Jinx, "He said he knew I would be alright. I remembered that when those bastards bum rushed me and he was right. I was okay when it was over."

"He was a friend of mine in a way. Neither of us were very popular. He would visit the Underworld on occasion. He always seemed sad but I guess knowing your own fate can do that to a person," said Flotsam pensively, "the Wild Boys will set a bonfire below in his honor tonight."

"Thank you for your help, Flotsam. We will not forget it, call on us if have need," I bowed.

"Your welcome and the same to you. You have leave to enter the Underworld," said Flotsam as she walked away, "just don't abuse the privilege."

"Yes, ma'am," I grimaced at her.

She threw her hand up once more and walked backed to her army of vagabonds. I took the chance to glance around again. The courtyard of City Hall was littered with hundreds of bodies, some alive and some dead. Heroes and medical personnel walked among the bodies, searching for injured survivors. From the main entrance of City Hall emerged a small knot of figures. The group began to walk around the battlefield, surveying the damage. I watched as they moved closer to my position. I recognized a few of the people, Thunderclap lead the pack with the Bubbler walking nearby. Floating behind was Shimmer, who seemed quite distracted amongst the carnage. I watched as Thunder stopped to talk to a group of heroes that included Interface. Interface gestured as he responded to Thunderclap and then he pointed in my direction. The group with Thunder turned as one to look at me and Shimmer raised his hand and floated over to me.

"Hello Tiger, good to see you still among the living," said Shimmer.

Shimmer glanced sidelong at the body of Flashback. He froze for a moment and slightly nodded his head. Blinking his eyes, which was pretty unnerving to watch, he turned and looked at me. He struggled with something for a moment then began speaking.

"Flashback says that the evil he warned you about is not what you just faced," said Shimmer, "but, he said you had already stared the evil in the face. What did he mean?"

"Wait a second, you mean that you were just talking to Flashback?" I stammered.

"Yes. I am dead, he is dead," answered the ghost, "it really isn't that hard to figure out, you know."

"Tell him that I'm sorry..." I began.

"It's too late," interrupted Shimmer, "he is already gone but, trust me, he knows."

I nodded as a lump rose in my throat. It really was a sad turn of events. The guy had known all along what he faced when he came to help save the city. He held the longest until help could arrive. He did it all without constant training, he did it from sheer will. And having determination when you know that you won't live to see victory is a hard thing. Bravery was doing what has to be done even if you were afraid to do it. Especially if you were too afraid...

Thunderclap and his entourage arrived to stand in front of my bruised and battered group. Looking us up and down, he saluted us all as did his companions. Gesturing to the battlefield, he began to speak.

"It was truly heroic to stand up against the forces of evil that so outnumbered all of us. The city thanks each and every one of you for your immeasurable service," began Thunderclap, "as a representat-"

"Can it loudmouth. I am too tired and that speech is too poorly delivered to listen to," I interrupted, "speaking of heroic actions, I didn't hear your patented thunder strike out here today."

"I was coordinating the defense from inside City Hall," stammered Thunderclap, "and I don't think a common street brawler has the right to say anything to me about leadership. Without me, City Hall would have fallen."

"Flashback did more to save City Hall today than you did," I said as I gestured at the broken body.

"Flashback? That coward from the eighties?" snarled Thunderclap.

A meaty smack sounded as I wiped the smug smile from his face. Thunder's head snapped back as he crumpled to the ground. Following through, I grabbed him up and slammed my fist into his face again. This time, blood splattered as his jaw snapped from the impact. I drew back to finish him off and an armored hand grabbed my arm and pulled me off him.

"That's enough, Tiger," said Junkyard from a thousand miles away.

"Damn right, it is!" said some nameless goon who was with Thunderclap, "We'll have you fired for this."

"No, you won't," I said as I reached for my belt, "because I quit."

Throwing my ID badge at Thunder's feet, I grinned evilly at the goon. My badge glinting in the slowly setting sun, I turned and walked away with stunned silence chasing me.

Urban Savagery

"As the cat lapses into savagery by night,
and barbarously explores the dark…"
—Frank Gelett Burgess

The city was teetering on the brink. Not much more chaos would be required to push it tumbling over the edge. The few citizens on the streets moved as if they were in a war zone, and rightly so. The legions of super villains that had escaped the Tower and attacked City Hall had lain waste to the neighborhoods they passed through. Even after they had been routed, the army of thugs had devastated anything that stood in the way of their headlong flight. They had ran as if the devil himself chased them and, like I said, after seeing what I had seen at the Tower he may have been.

Crossing the street, I could see the edge of my territory. My neighborhood looked as it usually did, very poor and rundown. Entering into my prowling grounds, I noticed that the destruction had not spread here. Obviously, there was no reason to come into Lowtown. No money to steal, no extortion rackets, no black market, basically there was nothing to draw them here. The funny thing was that Lowtown looked better than any other area of the city now.

Seeing a few people out and about, I made sure that they knew about the troubles in the city and to keep close to home. Just in case. Continuing on, I eventually reached my apartment building. Some people would call it a tenemant. Entering the building, I nodded at the fat desk clerk. He looked pastier than usual.

"Damn, what da hell is going on out dere?" he exclaimed, his accent thick from anxiety, "I've been watching da news all day, it looks like da end of da world."

"You don't know the half of it," I replied as I walked to the stairwell, "make peace with your gods today, fat boy. There may not be a tomorrow."

He paled even more when what I said began to sink in. I turned my back on him and began trudging up the stairs. After getting my ass kicked by Darkfall and then being manhandled by the Lost Boys and later buried in a tidal wave of punks, I was a bit worn out to say the least. My legs felt like rubber and they burned like acid with every step I took. My lungs couldn't expand fully, maybe broken ribs. Short of breath, I finally reached my floor and woodenly opened the metal door.

As I stepped in the hall, I could smell fresh cigarette smoke. While most people's nose curled at the smell, it didn't really bother me. In fact, with my heightened senses, cigarette smoke was an improvement over some people's natural body odor. This time, however, the person in question didn't need any help. She had the most enticing body odor I had ever smelled.

Michelle stood beside my door, smoking and looking fidgety. When the door closed behind me, she turned at the noise. Throwing her cigarette aside, she ran towards me with a sheen of tears in her eyes. Slamming into me harder than some of the thugs I had fought today, she could only sob as she clung to me.

"I saw you on TV," she sniffled, "it looked like there were thousands of them and you were the only hero there."

"There were a few others, darling," I said in an attempt to calm her down.

"Well, I didn't see them. I thought they were going to kill you," she said between gasping breaths.

"They nearly did but I am here now," I replied, "a little worse for wear but okay."

Pulling away from me with a shocked look, Michelle blushed and tried to stammer some sort of apology. I smiled and brushed a stray tear from her flushed cheeks before I shushed her with a single finger over her lips. Putting my arm around her, more for support than I would like to admit, I handed her my key ring as I let her guide me to my place. Sliding my key in the lock, she pushed the door open with her foot and we squeezed into my apartment.

It was a mess. I had planned to have a normal day at work and come home in time to clean up. So much for those plans. On my table was a stack of letters, mostly bills, and a pyramid of cans. Coca Cola cans, thank you, I don't drink anymore but I am still a slob. Dirty laundry lay in every place but the clothes hamper. Take out boxes surrounded the floor around my recliner. My bed sheets were crumpled at the foot of my bed and looked as if I hadn't changed them in a week. In fact, I hadn't changed them in two weeks but who's counting?

"Sorry, I meant to clean up before you came over," I apologized.

"Don't worry about it. I have a seven year old daughter," she smiled, "this is nothing."

"No, it's a total mess. But thanks anyway," I said with a grin and a shrug.

Pulling me to the bathroom, Michelle sat me down on the toilet and began to draw a hot bath. I kept my eyes closed, I didn't want to contemplate what it looked like in here. Michelle got up and left the bathroom. I could hear her fumbling around in the kitchen for a minute. When she returned, I opened my eyes in time to see her pouring the contents of my salt shaker in the water. Turning off the tap, she motioned to the tub.

"Get in. A hot salt bath is what you need right now," she commanded.

"Umm, a little privacy?" I said sheepishly.

Chuckling, she shut the door as she left the room. I slowly and painfully undressed as steam poured up from the hot bath. Taking my time, I was able to remove my costume with only a few winces. Picking my foot up, I dipped a single toe into the slightly cloudy water.

"DAMN, THAT'S HOT!"

I leapt back and shook my foot to try to lessen the pain. Michelle called through the door admonishing me to not be such a big baby and didn't I fight super villains for a living? I didn't feel like arguing about

---

whether I *still* did so I just glared at the door instead. Trying again, I was able to keep my toe in long enough to try for a whole foot. About a minute later, I was trying to sit down in the pool of lava that Michelle called a bath. For the record, the sitting down is the worst part of the entire process, hot or cold.

Finally, I was totally immersed and began to slowly relax. The hot water was no longer intolerable and it was loosening my taut muscles. The steam and heat made me break out in a mild sweat and my eyelids began to droop. As I was drifting off to sleep, I could hear Michelle moving around in the apartment. Floating…

When I awoke, I had no idea where I was for a minute. I had been asleep for so long the warm was cold and my skin was pasty and wrinkled. Shivering as I stood, I grabbed a towel and wrapped it around me as I stepped out of the tub. Rubbing vigorously, I occasionally twitched as I hit a sore spot with the towel. Finally dried off, I grabbed my gray bathrobe and slipped it on. Opening the bathroom door, I walked into a room I didn't recognize.

"How long was I in there?" I asked after staring at what used to be my apartment.

The floor was spotless. There were no clothes on the floor and the hamper was empty. My bed was made with fresh clean sheets. The take out boxes and other assorted trash had been removed. The air had that pine tree smell that comes from industrial strength cleaners. Hell, even the dust had been wiped off my TV screen and that was a first!

"About an hour and a half," said Michelle from the kitchen, "have a seat and I will bring you some dinner. It's almost done cooking."

"Dinner?" I said dumfounded, "Michelle, sweetie, you didn't have to do that."

"Well, we do have a dinner date tonight," she said as she stepped into sight brandishing a wooden spoon with a coating of red sauce, "and I didn't think you would be up for Solicito's. So, I made us some spaghetti."

"My world famous spaghetti." she added with a wink as she twirled back into the kitchen.

Sitting down in my recliner, I leaned back and could smell some sort of fragrance on the upholstery. I couldn't identify it but it smelled really nice, whatever it was. Resting my hand on the armrest, I noticed that Michelle had found my remote control and placed it in reach. Grabbing it from the end table, I turned on the television.

Every channel had coverage of the rioting villains rampaging through the streets. Picking a single channel, I settled in to watch from the sidelines this time. The station I had picked was showing live footage from Crystal Lake, one of the more affluent sections of the city. It looked like it had been bombed. None of the buildings shown had an intact set of windows and most cars were burning or vandalized in some way. The pavement was literally shattered in places, resembling impact craters. The camera panned around to focus on a group of heroes fighting a much larger force of villains. Some bubble headed loudmouth was yammering some nonsense about the civil unrest being caused by economic disparity but I was less interested in psychobabble and more interested in the fate of the heroes. I recognized a couple of them.

On the screen, I could see Flaming Demon and Straight Arrow fighting a losing battle alongside a few heroes I didn't know. As I watched, Demon was lashing out at a wall of snarling punks with a flaming trident. Straight Arrow stood behind him, firing arrows at an eye blurring pace. The other heroes were fighting for all their worth but eventually they just were not enough of them. One hero, dressed in mostly black, stumbled and was overran by the mob. Savagely, the enraged villains slaughtered him and fell upon Demon. I saw him kill at least three of them before he was impaled upon his own weapon. The other three heroes broke and ran as Arrow laid down cover fire. The mob shied away from his barrage at first but quickly overcame their fear and charged him. He threw his bow at them in a futile gesture of defiance before they crushed him. Those were my friends…

Michelle walked into the room carrying a steaming plate of noodles and sauce. It had smelled delicious when she was cooking it but now, all I could smell, taste, and feel was rage. She took one look at me and set the plate down. Grabbing my face in her warm, soft hands, she turned my face up towards her. Kissing me softly on the lips, she stroked my check gently.

"Go," she whispered, "but come back to me. I will be here waiting for you."

I looked deep into her eyes and saw her fear reflected back at me. Smiling sadly at her, I nodded. Standing, I grabbed both her hands and pulled her towards me. Hugging her fiercely, it was all I could do to eventually let go.

"I will," I said, "I promise."

Stepping away from her, I walked to my closest and pulled the door open. Pushing aside my street clothes, I reached for my costume. I grabbed an empty hanger. Pulling it out, I stared at it for a minute and began to search the bottom of the closet. What the hell?

"Oh! I forgot!" said Michelle as she hustled into the kitchen.

She came back with my costume over her arm. She also carried my new gloves from my other suit. I looked at her with a question in my eyes.

"There was a hole in it. And the gloves you were wearing were different from the one on this suit," she explained as she held up my spare costume.

"You know, a man could get used to this sort of treatment," I said.

"Don't," she replied with a devilish look in her eyes, "I'm just setting the hook."

"You did that days ago. You're already reeling," I replied.

"Am I?" she said sweetly as she held my suit out to me.

"You know you are, beautiful," I said as I took it.

Winking at her, I walked into the bathroom to get ready. Our light banter had taken the edge off for a minute, but spending a few minutes gearing up brought the tensions back. My bravado aside, I had the funny feeling that I wouldn't make it through the night. I was in my element stalking and catching street thugs. Open warfare was not my forte. Working out everyday and practicing martial arts was no match for rampaging armies of super powered thugs and angry, weapon toting, gang bangers. Popping my claws, I watched the glint of the light bulb play on their razor edges.

"Powers or not, a lot are going down with me tonight," I whispered the promise.

Retracting the blades, I walked out of the bathroom. I had entered as a average everyday man in a bathrobe, I left as an armored warrior of justice. Meeting Michelle's worried eyes with my own steel gaze, I smiled bravely at her.

"Wait for me," I said.

Turning before she could reply, I walked from the apartment. Reaching the stairwell, I bounded down two steps at a time. Hitting the bottom floor running, I burst through the steel door. The fat desk clerk was still there and he nearly jumped out of his skin when I sped into the room. Stopping before him, I turned to look him in the face.

"Stand tall," I said, "if anyone comes in here trying to start trouble, use that street cannon of yours. Don't hesitate."

Gesturing at the shotgun I knew he kept under the desk, I nodded grimly. He stared back at me and for a moment his back straightened. For a moment, he looked like the man he could have been had he not taken the path most men take, the easy path. He set his lips firmly and nodded back at me.

"Yes sir," he said in a firm voice.

At that, I left the building and jogged down the street. It wasn't hard to know where to go. Even in the relative calm of my neighborhood, I could hear the sounds of battle. Two blocks up and one over I thought. I can make it in under two minutes. I hope that isn't too late.

Jogging as fast as I could and still retain the ability to fight effectively, I ate up the distance to the fight even quicker than I had estimated. Rounding a corner, I encountered my first skirmish of the early evening. A dozen Weathermen were attacking a trio of heroes, two females and one male. The Weathermen were all punks who had exhibited various storm powers. Currently, they were throwing lightning bolts and calling down intense pockets of wind and rain. The trio of heroes were responding well and holding their own. The male was firing beams of energy from his eyes, striking a Weatherman with each shot. The dark skinned heroine was leaping about attacking multiple thugs with a pair of slender daggers. The other woman was standing with her hands to her head as a pair of gang bangers fought each other in front of her. No claws needed this time.

I was going to try to not commit wholesale slaughter tonight. Adrenaline had driven me into a frenzy today and the deaths of my friends had fueled the fires of my rage. But anger and rage were not what I needed. Calm detachment was what enabled me to fight villains many times more powerful than me. Controlling my emotions while those around me lost hold of theirs had saved me more than once. I needed that detachment back. This would be good practice for it.

Striding into the street, I simply laid out the first punk I got near with a vicious right cross. Two others turned and looked at me and began to slightly edge back. Suddenly they didn't like the odds as much. I lifted my arm and pointed at them as I stared at their slightly familiar eyes.

"Run."

Amazingly they did and when those two turned tail, the others quickly followed their example. Out of breath, the trio of heroes walked over to me. The guy hunkered down on his haunches and stared at the pavement. The two ladies had an almost shell-shocked look. Obviously, these three were used to the safer sections of the city.

"Catch your breath," I said, "it's gonna be a long night."

"Thanks for the assist," said the guy as he looked up at me, "call me Sunbeam"

"Yeah, we were doing okay but every bit helps," said the dark skinned heroine.

"What Stiletto means to say is it was damn good to see you," said the other woman, "Vertigo is my name. Pretty impressive, what you did back there. I've never seen Weathermen run away like that."

"Oh, I think those two knew me from a little while back," I grinned, "in fact, I am almost positive of it."

"So, what's the plan?" interrupted Stiletto.

"You tell me. I'm a civilian," I said.

"My ass, you are," said Sunbeam. "you're the Night Tiger."

I stared at him blankly for a moment. His tone indicated that there was more to this than just one hero recognizing another. Sunbeam turned to Vertigo with a puzzled look in his face.

"He doesn't know, man," said Vertigo, "after you put Thunderclap in the hospital, one of his flunkies wanted to put out a warrant for your arrest. The government liaison, Blizzard, showed up. Once he heard the whole story of the defense of the city and who really led it, he was a bit upset at Thunderclap."

"You are reinstated," added Sunbeam, "I think they are going to promote you too."

"Great, more bad news," I smirked.

"Ha! So, like I asked a minute ago, what's the plan boss?" said Stiletto.

"We follow the noise," I said as I zeroed in on the sounds of violence and became to trot up the street.

The other heroes fell into place behind me. Stiletto catching up to me and matching me stride for stride while Vertigo and Sunbeam flew beside us. Minutes later, we crossed into Diamond Run. Diamond Run was the financial section of the city. All the rich stock brokerages had offices here. At the moment, the buildings were being ravaged by the Anarchists. The Anarchists were a gang that specialized in attacking various pillars of civilization in hopes of bringing mankind back to an age of anarchy. Like mankind needs any help with that...

Revolution, leader of the Anarchists, was marching down the street directing his minions to destroy this building and that one. Fortunately, ordering members of the Anarchists to do something was like herding cats and most of the fools did whatever met their twisted little fancies. A single hero stood on the street. He was a skinny little guy who was carrying a really big and fancy gun. He was laying down a barrage of fire from the gun that was mowing down anarchists left and right. Anytime an enemy would get near him, he would twist a dial on his belt and disappear for a split second only to reappear nearby.

Signaling the heroes with me, I charged straight for Revolution. Behind me, I could hear the trio doing their part in the battle. Reaching my quarry before he noticed my approach, I flattened him from behind. Not real sporting, I know. He hit the pavement hard and a few anarchists near him whipped around in response.

I laid into them with a vengeance. They lacked any real training, they were too individualistic to ever submit to a fighting school. The few that I had engaged went down quickly and easily. Looking around, the other heroes had pretty much wrapped up the remaining anarchists. Seeing the four of them standing together, I felt the slow blossoming of pride. They were surviving a trial by fire and were doing a fairly respectable job of it.

"C'mon," I said, "we're just getting started."

We moved as a group through Diamond Run. I knew where we were going now. Crystal Lake. It was one place that I knew was having a lot of problems. Both Demon and Arrow had been "A" list heroes. That meant that when the world was about to end, they were some of the heroes you would expect to show up and save the day. That wouldn't be happening anymore. The "A" list was getting shorter by the minute.

A block from the edge of Crystal Lake, we near the D. R. Law Enforcement Station. It had been hit hard during the initial riots. Several large holes were visible in the outside wall. A large circle of sandbags protected a pair of heroes from another group of Anarchists. The Anarchists looked almost comical in their uncoordinated attempts to breach the station. Without rhyme or reason, a few would charge the bunker and get easily repulsed.

Looking over at the slender hero, called Gun Control, I pointed at the main group of dumbasses. "Think you can hit them with rubber bullets from here and get their attention?"

"I have something better," he grinned, "watch out, I don't know what this will do."

He grabbed a fist sized canister from one of his various belt pouches. Pulling a silver pin, he counted to three and lobbed it in a high arc. When the canister was about ten feet above the heads of the villains, it exploded with a modest "pop". Suddenly, the Anarchists were running away waving their hands above their heads. The other Anarchists spun at the noise and commotion and were taken from behind as the heroes behind the sandbags attacked.

"I've been waiting to try that out," grinned Gun Control triumphantly.

"What the hell was it?" asked Stiletto

"It's a "bouncy ball" grenade," he explained, "you know those bouncy balls you can buy for a quarter from the machines in grocery stores? Well, that grenade has hundreds of smaller balls made of the same material. They are supposed to feel like being stung by a hundred bees at once. Yet at the same time, remain as non-lethal as possible."

"You got anymore?" I asked.

"Plenty, among other cool toys," grinned the young hero, "wait until you see my skunk grenade. I got the idea from talking to Stink Bomb."

"No thanks," I replied, "I had to smell him every morning. I don't need a reminder."

As we were talking, we had began to walk towards the Station. The heroes from the bunker regarded us wearily. Dark circles were under both of their eyes and they looked like warmed over death. Judging from the number of injured and dead punks in this neighborhood, I can imagine it had been as tough as these two made it seem from their appearance. And that was pretty rough.

"Thanks for the assist," said one hero in a gold uniform.

"No problem. What's the situation here?" I said.

"Real bad. Me and Roughneck were the only heroes on duty here. Those crazy guys have been tearing up the place and all we could do was hide in here," said the hero.

"Yeah, there were just too many of them. There was a...a guy. He looked like a banker...They..." said Roughneck, "They ripped him apart and laughed while doing it."

"There wasn't anything you could do," I said, Even though it wasn't true. They could have acted like heroes and maybe things would have been different. Yeah, I thought, they could have been ripped apart too.

"Listen, you need to hold together. We can turn the tide tonight but we have to all start acting like heroes," I said, "especially me."

"Man, without you none of us would've made this far," said Sunbeam.

"Listen, if I had not had a temper tantrum earlier today, you may not have needed help in the first place," I said while shaking my head.

"That doesn't matter now," said Stiletto, "we need a leader and, unfortunately, that means you."

The other heroes chuckled for a minute as I grinned at the sassy black girl. Nothing more fun to have around than a sassy black girl, they'll tell you how you are screwing up in a heartbeat.

"Fine," I said, "then somebody get on the horn and find out what's going on. Diamond Run is as clear as possible for now. We are going into Crystal Lake."

"I don't need to get on the horn to tell you about Crystal Lake," said Roughneck, "it's overrun."

"Call anyway," I said, "I need to know if anyone is headed there or if it's been written off."

"It's probably written off," he replied.

"You had better hope it isn't," I smiled, "because if it is, we are definitely going."

"What? You're crazy!" he exclaimed.

"No, I refuse to abandon the innocent people of this city to a mob of killers," I said with a gravelly voice, "if you want to leave them for dead then you need to find somebody else to run with."

"No. No, you're right," he said as he began to go into the station, "sorry, I'll get right on it."

Roughneck walked into the building. I continued to stare at him until he was gone from my sight. There was just something about "country club" heroes that pissed me off royally. Turning to look at the others, I had to suppress a groan. Judging by the way these junior leaguers were looking at me, there was no way I was going to get out of being leader.

"You," I said as I pointed at the guy in gold, "what's your name?"

"Triage. I am a healer," he said, "for instance, you have three broken ribs, a broken left pinkie knuckle, several deep bruises, twisted right ank—"

"Okay, I get the point. And every time you list a body part, it starts hurtin'!" I said with a grimace.

Triage raised his hands above his head. Golden light that matched the color of his costume flowed over me. Almost instantly my aches and pains went away. The absence of pain was almost as shocking as actually being injured. Shocked or not, the healing energy rejuvenated me and for the first time today I felt almost human. The glow ended abruptly as he staggered and fell to his knees. Bounding to his side, I grabbed his elbow.

"Are you okay?" I asked.

Shaking his head and gasping for breath, he looked up at me. Lines etched his face as he grimaced horribly. Tears flowed freely down his checks. His legs were quivering and his hands were shaky.

"I'll be all right in a second," he said after a few moments, "when I heal someone, I take their pain. It has to go somewhere and so it goes into me."

Pulling himself upright, he looked at me as the pain subsided. "Don't worry. You were nothing. Roughneck in there almost killed me earlier. He went after those bastards when they were killing the banker. They nearly ripped him apart. Only the police drones saved him. He crawled away from them."

Shaking his head, Triage stumbled slightly as he began to walk into the station. He bumped into the doorframe as he passed from inside. Maybe I had been wrong about those two. Heroes can come in all sorts of packages.

"Stiletto, you and Sunbeam post watch for now," I said as I began to walk towards the station. Stopping suddenly, Vertigo nearly collided with me. Turning around, I pointed at her. "On second thought, you take Stiletto's place. I want her inside with me. I don't trust her."

"What? Why?" asked Stiletto.

"If they come back, I don't trust you to leave any bad guys for me!" I said as I walked inside.

The inside of the D. R. station was immaculate. Marble floors with gold flecks matched the white columns running down the middle of the room. Soft, pleasant lighting showcased the tasteful décor. Comfortable leather chairs sat next to mahogany tables. Roughneck was visible through the door of the communication center. Triage stood next to a water cooler drinking from a paper cone. Crumpling up the cup and tossing it in a nearby wastebasket, he walked over to us.

"Night Tiger, sir? The conference room is this way. Roughneck will bring us all the information when he gets it." said the hero as he motioned to a nearby door. Amazingly, the plague on the door said "Conference Room". Some superhero detective I am.

"Don't call me sir," I said.

Grinning at him, I walked into the room. A long table dominated the middle of the room. A pair of computer stations were located on the far wall. The outside wall had a long bank of television sets. Several were on and broadcasting news reports from different stations. Walking to grab the seat at the head of the table, I noticed that a control panel was located near it. Sitting down in the chair, I examined the panel as the other heroes filed in behind me. It looked simple enough and I pressed a button to make a single station be broadcast. Instantly, the screens had began to show a large version of the station I had chosen. Pressing the button again, the screens began showing all the stations again.

While I had been fiddling with the remote control, the others had taken their seats. I looked down the table at them, the three of them were staring at me expectantly. Here is where the "leader" part of me had to take over. The problem was, I was just making this stuff up as I went along. I had no idea what I was doing.

"Look. You guys are doing a hell of a job. All of you," I said.

As I began to speak, Roughneck walked in the door with a couple of sheets of paper in his hand. He waited until I finished my sentence and then stepped up to hand the papers. Taking them, I began to read them. Damn.

Chaos reigned over the city. The national guard were outside town building a makeshift prison camp, too scared to come in and help. Entire neighborhoods were under control of some of the bigger gangs. The Hellions held Aztec Terrace and the Gateway mall. A strike force of heroes lead by Jinx were fighting hard there. The Arachnids were controlling the Foundry, the industrial section. Junkyard had taken a team to handle them. Crystal Lake was under attack by an heretofore unknown group. Blizzard was mobilizing some heroes but wouldn't be there anytime soon.

"The situation is this," I said, "Crystal Lake is defending itself from an unidentified force of villains. There is nobody but us who can make it there in time to make a difference. I want the automatic defense for this station activated. I want everyone to prep for battle."

Standing up, I dropped the papers on the tabletop. "Notify the others, we leave in five minutes."

100

I walked out of the room, the door shutting behind me. Walking across the station, I pushed open the stairwell door. Jogging up the stairs, I quickly reached the third floor. Walking across the balcony, I opened the roof door. Stepping out on the roof, I could see a few police drones as they buzzed by. Small circular objects, they had a small computer brain and a big stun cannon. They were, however, limited in the number of shots they could fire at a given time and they took a long time to identify a threat.

Walking across the roof, I looked around the skyline. Flames were visible to my east, the direction of Crystal Lake. To the north, the city was quiet. To the south, I could hear loud explosions and see towers of light rising to the heavens. To the west, I could see small specks flying about each other. They were heroes and villains locked in combat, but flying through the night at such a distance that they could barely be seen. I glanced back towards Crystal Lake but for some reason my eyes kept being drawn back to the north. Why was it so quiet there?

My musing over with, I left the roof and descended the stairs and walked out the front door of the building. Standing outside, the heroes were on edge. Triage and Roughneck stood near each other talking quietly. Gun Control was fiddling with his gun and ignoring everything else. Vertigo and Sunbeam warily scanned the open street in front of them. Only Stiletto was outwardly calm but even she couldn't resist twirling her blades as she stood by herself. When I exited the building, they all seemed to perk up and pay attention.

"Let's move out," I said.

We all set off to the east, making good speed towards our destination. The closer we got, the more destruction we saw. Passing an empty intersection, we crossed over into the outer edge of Crystal Lake.

Burned out sandbag bunkers contained the bodies of privately hired security forces. Smoking ruins were all that remained of the mercenary guards. To the left of the bunkers was a small, well manicured park. In the center of the round patch of nature was a trio of shapes that were ominous in the deep shadows. Moving towards the shapes, I noticed one of them move and signaled to my team for them to be careful. Stepping close enough to see the shapes clearly, I froze.

The shapes were three heroes who had been impaled upon stakes. One of them was still alive and twitching slightly. I glanced at Triage and raised one eyebrow in a questioning look. His small shake of the head and his expression told me all I needed to know. There was nothing we could do for him.

Stepping up to the delirious and nearly unconscious man, I stood motionless for a moment. Slowly, I popped my claws and as swiftly and gently as I could, I sliced through his throat. He gurgled once, then twice, and then he was gone. I stood there for a minute, trying to make sense of my world. But there was no comfort to be had.

Triage put his hand on my shoulder and guided me away from the corpses. "You did the right thing. It was a hard thing but a right one. He would have suffered for hours."

"That doesn't make it easier," I said grimly, "the kid gloves are off now. Vertigo, can you find who did this?"

"I don't know, but I am feeling a large concentration of hate and rage a couple of blocks that way," she answered as she pointed through the trees.

"Okay, then that is the way we are headed. It's time for a little payback," I snarled, "these animals have taken it too far."

The Widening Gyre

"The darkness drops again; but now I know
That twenty centuries of stony sleep
Were vexed to nightmare by a rocking cradle,"
—William Butler Yeats, The Second Coming

The seven of us stalked through the sparse forest and burst onto a street that appeared deserted. The sounds of violent battle came from the next street over. Hurrying across the road, we all tried to stay as low as possible. We would have looked hilarious if it hadn't been so dangerous out here. Staying in the shadows of an alleyway, we picked our way carefully towards the sounds of skirmish.

An old man in a bathrobe stood in the middle of the street in front of a large white house. On the lawn of the house was a small group of people watching. The old man was surrounded by a ring of villains four people deep. They taunted and struck at him whenever he turned his back to them. To his credit, they were obviously too scared of him to get too close. Eventually, one of the punks got careless and showed us why. The old man turned on the villain before he could back away. The old man grabbed the punk up in one hand and threw him thirty feet through the air. The punk landed with a sickening splat and didn't get up. This riled the punks up even more and they began to press closer to the old man. That was a mistake.

Once the punks got a step too close, the old man began to tear into them. They were too tightly packed and too close to him to escape.

Within a minute, enough of the villains were flat on the ground to convince the others that a less well guarded house might be a safer target. They broke and ran.

We had only been in the alley for about two minutes before the old man had routed three dozen punks. Pretty impressive for someone who should be in a walker right now. Motioning with my head, me and my team exited the alley and headed towards the old man. As we got close, he noticed us and spun to face us.

"Back fer more, eh?" said the old guy, "Well, I'll show you nazis what an american fights like…"

"Whoa there, old fella," I said with my hands up in a submissive gesture, "we are the good guys."

The old guy stared at us for a minute with a fierce look in his eyes. Suddenly his eyes began to cloud over and he seemed almost lost. He looked around as if he couldn't find something important, something that mattered. One of the people on the lawn came down to his side quickly. It was a teenage boy, about fifteen.

"Sorry, grandfather has episodes sometimes where he thinks it is 1944," said the boy as he looped his arm through his grandfather's. The old man looked up at the taller boy with a real expression of gratitude on his face.

"Thank you, Sparrow," said the old man.

"He thinks I am his sidekick Sparrow," blushed the boy.

"Wait," I said, "Sparrow. You mean he is the American Eagle? The superhero from World War two?"

"Yep, that's my grandfather," said the boy with pride., "he can't remember who he is most days, it's good to see someone else remember who he was."

"He's a legend," said Gun Control.

"Well, I had better get him inside. The noises from the battles are causing him to have his episodes. In times like this, we have a room with reinforced steel walls for him to stay in," explained the boy.

Pulling on the old man's arm, the boy was able to move him a few feet before the old man's eyes gained a gleam of misguided intelligence. Jerking free of the boy, the old man stepped away from him and took up a fighting stance. Throwing a thunderous blow, the old man's fist rocketed towards the slight boy. The boy simply held up his own hand and caught the hurtling fist. Pulling the old man to him, the boy hugged him firmly but gently.

"It's okay, grandpa. We are going inside now," said the boy as he picked the old man up in his arms like a baby.

Catching my eye, the boy spoke, "Are you here to fight the people tearing up this place? The people who attacked my family?"

"Yes," I replied evenly.

"Then give me a minute and I will be back out here," said the boy as he turned towards the house.

It actually took seven minutes. The boy came out of the house wearing a red, white, and blue costume that looked fifty years old. Seeing my amused look, the boy grinned sheepishly.

"It was my grandfather's from the war," he said.

"It's an appropriate costume for the new American Eagle," said Vertigo with an encouraging smile, "your grandfather would be proud."

"Well, after this is over, I'm getting a new one," said the boy as he eyed the costumes of the other heroes.

"I wouldn't change it much if I were you. There is something powerful about it," I said.

A loud explosion a few blocks away cut short the fashion show and we all headed towards the sound. Stepping onto the busiest street in Crystal Lake, I got my first real life view of the army of punks that I had seen killing heroes on TV. They were tearing into high class stores and stealing everything that could carry. And some stuff they couldn't.

I was about to signal the attack when a commotion started behind the mob of villains. Stepping back, I pushed my team into the shadow of a stairwell. The mob of villains split like the Red Sea. Marching down the gap were eight beings. I recognized a few, one was Battlefield. He had killed my old classmate Cobra in cold blood. Another was Darkfall, still limping slightly from our run-in earlier. I wonder how he escaped the demon. Five others passed that were unfamiliar to me but literally exuded raw power. The last villain was a surprise. Primal brought up the rear, his every step an exercise in force.

The assembly of villains began to cheer as the line of figures passed through them. Several of the eight supervillains would wave or gesture at the crowds of thugs. Eventually all had passed and turned left down a side street before they reached us. Lucky for us. Eight supervillains working together was really bad news for everyone involved.

"Give them a minute to pass out of earshot," I said, "we can't take on all those thugs and the big guys at the same time."

"They didn't look that tough," said Stiletto, "we can take 'em."

"That one in the black leather jacket has nearly killed me twice in the past week," I grinned, "and this time he brought seven friends."

"So did you!" replied Stiletto.

"Yeah, but I would still like to have a distinct advantage when we go after those guys," I explained, "if there are enough of us, they may just surrender."

"Oh yeah, those guys looked like the surrendering type for sure," interjected Roughneck

"Point taken," I said, "but it don't matter now. We are in the clear."

I felt I had given enough time for the supervillains to move far enough away. I split the team into groups of two. After they had formed up into teams, I gave them the plan. Roughneck and Eagle would charge the mob. Sunbeam and Gun Control would lay down as much cover fire as possible. Stiletto and I would work the edges of the villains and Vertigo and Triage would hang back and give support. Giving the "go" signal, I didn't check to see if Stil was following me as I slipped down the sidewalk towards the enemy.

Getting as near as I safely could, I looked back to see how the team had deployed. Gun Control was in a fire escape above the stairwell we had hidden in. Sunbeam sprinted across the street, climbed a short set of steps, and crouched in a doorway. Feeling a presence approaching, I noticed Stiletto creeping up behind me in the gloom. I whistled.

Suddenly, American Eagle and Roughneck were running directly at the mass of villains. Eagle looked almost ludicrous with his slender body and decades old costume. Roughneck, on the other hand, looked normal with his first step, by the third he was six inches taller and long black hair had quickly began to grow all over his body. By the time the two were halfway to the thugs, Roughneck looked like a seven foot tall were-monster. He let out a bloodcurdling howl as he plunged into the mass of gangbangers. Eagle tried to give a battle cry as he attacked but his adolescent voice betrayed him, cracking and breaking midway through the yell.

The moment that Roughneck had howled the first time, Gun Control was sighting his outlandish rifle. As Eagle's broken cry rose up from the melee, six villains had already been taken down by silent shots from the weapon. Sunbeam began hurling blasts of solar radiation, blinding and burning with each burst. His power stunned the thugs that it didn't directly hit and incapacitated the ones it did.

Stiletto and I slipped to the side of the mob as they were concentrated on the two heavy hitters in their midst. Nodding at her, I extended my claws as she drew her silver daggers. Both of us leapt at the bad guys at the same time. She spinning and slashing, me leaping and striking, we both were cutting through these losers like a hot knife through butter.

Not be left out, I could see the obvious golden glow of Triage's healing power bathing Roughneck. I could also see several of the punks wandering around in a daze and I knew that Vertigo was working her will on them as well.

It took less than a minute before the punks that had encircled us suddenly found themselves outnumbered and surrounded. Several threw their hands up in surrender and my team formed up around them. A few still wanted to fight but a concentrated attack from all of us disabused them of that notion.

"What are we going to do with these?" asked Triage as he healed our minor wounds.

"I have something for them," said Gun Control.

He stepped forward and lowered his weapon at the captives. The punks had a look of creeping terror on their faces as soon as the weapon was pointed in their direction. Grinning, the hero pulled the trigger on the big gun and held it down. A spray of blue chemical streamed from a nozzle on the underside of the main rifle barrel. The liquid coated the thugs and solidified as it made contact. The half a dozen thugs still standing tried to escape the spray of liquid. Bumping into and pushing aside each other, they quickly began to slow as the liquid dried in the night air. Before they could comprehend what was going on, they were all glued to each other in a blue sticky mass.

"It's a glue gun," said Gun Control as he indicated the small nozzle and tank it was attached too, "the adhesive will last about two hours and it takes vast strength to break free of it until it degrades."

"How vast?" I asked as I grinned at the struggling villains.

"More than any of them, even if they all worked together," he answered.

"Well, Tiger, do you think it will work on me?" said Primal's voice behind me.

We had been set up. The supervillains that had passed a few minutes before had us surrounded. They either doubled back or had known we were there all along. The mob of punks had been bait to get us to attack. How could I have been so stupid?

"I guess we will have to find out, asshole," I said as I leapt at Primal.

Answering my leap with one of his own, Darkfall came flying out of the shadows and we impacted in midair. As we fell to the ground, thrashing wildly, Primal charged at the two of us. A slender figure intercepted him and began to throw punches. I couldn't see the rest of the team but I could hear powers activating and cries of pain.

If Darkfall had been arrogant the first time we fought and royally pissed the second time, this time he was insane. Flailing with all his might, he was so out of control that he was hardly even damaging me. Obviously, I had pushed this particular villain too far. Let's see how much further I could push him...

"You fight like a bitch!" I grinned as I rammed my forehead into his teeth.

He howled as his teeth shattered, spraying blood and chunks of enamel. Grabbing his throat, I retracted my claws before they slashed his jugular. Pressing down hard on his throat, I squeezed until Darkfall slipped into sleepy time. Crawling off of his unconscious body, I quickly looked around.

Eagle and Primal were fighting it out, each powerful blow sounding like a cannon shot. Gun Control was firing erratically at the villain called Battlefield who was returning fire with cannons attached to his wristbands. Vertigo and a dark skinned man were locked into some sort of staring contest. Triage was backing away from a evil looking villain carrying a long sword. Roughneck was battling with some sort of tall gargoyle reptile-looking monster, both savagely mauling each other. Sunbeam was being throttled by a tall thug with tendrils of smoke wafting around him. Stiletto was locked into a dance of flashing blades and whirling bodies with the last villain, a man wielding some crazy silver chain that moved as if it was alive.

Grabbing a chunk of brick from the sidewalk, I threw my best fastball at the guy choking Sunbeam. The brick struck Sunbeam's attacker in the back of the head and dropped him on the spot. Lifting painfully onto his elbow, Sunbeam blasted the swordsman stalking Triage. I ran at Battlefield. I had a bit of a score to settle with him. Leaping into the air, I snap kicked him in the back of the head with all my strength. He rocked forward slightly and turned to look at me. Sucker.

Gun Control fired a strange projectile that hummed as it cut through the air. It struck Battlefield's exposed back and attached itself to his armor. Blue lighting suddenly erupted from the small cylinder and raced around the villain. For a few seconds, Battlefield twitched and shivered as the energy coursed through him. Then the blue glow dissipated and the villain crumpled to the ground.

"What was that?" I asked Gun Control

"My taser round," answered the hero as he applied sticky foam to the unconscious Battlefield, "extra strength."

"I like it," I grinned, "remind me to talk to you after this is all over."

"Roger that," he replied.

The only heroes still locked in combat were American Eagle, Vertigo, Stiletto, and Roughneck. The rest of us moved in to help. I slugged the guy staring down Vertigo and he dropped like a rock. Gun Control shot a few tranquilizer rounds into the lizardman fighting Roughneck and within a minute the big creature was sleeping. Sunbeam took careful aim and blasted the whip out of the hand of the man fighting Stiletto. Suddenly disarmed, the asshole tried to run and was knocked down by a leaping Roughneck.

Finally, Primal and American Eagle were left throwing punches that shook the sidewalk. With each blow they threw, the sidewalk shook and windows shattered. None of us were in the league of those two, if we stepped into one of those punches it would probably kill us. Remembering Primal's weakness, I slipped over to a panting Vertigo and whispered into her ear. She shook her head.

"Sorry, I am wiped out," she said, "the battle with Brainstorm over there drained me. I'll have to sleep before I can use my powers again."

"No worries," I said, "I'll think of something."

Bullshit, I would. I had no idea what to do. Primal was stronger and way more experienced than his teenaged opponent. Eagle was holding his own but he wouldn't last much longer. Primal had centuries of practice in his favor.

"Boy, your grandfather couldn't beat me in the forties," taunted Primal, "and you can't do it now."

"He told me about you," panted the boy, "he said you were a nancy. What does that mean?"

Primal snarled and lifted both fists above his head. He brought them crashing down towards Eagle but the boy dodged to the left. Primal continued the motion and sank his hands a few inches into the sidewalk. Ripping up a section of the concrete, he swept it to the left and knocked Eagle off his feet. Grabbing the boy, he picked him up and hurled him through a brick wall.

Laughing, he turned to us and waded into our midst. A backhanded fist struck me and knocked me twenty feet. My kevlar armor shattered upon impact and shards buried themselves into my shoulder. Gun Control unleashed round after round into the villain to no avail. Sunbeam hurled bursts of energy at him but he just laughed. Roughneck leapt at Primal and the villain plucked him out of the air and slammed him to the ground. He then reached down and picked up the shape shifter's still form. Spinning, Primal hurled Roughneck into Sunbeam and Gun Control. Both heroes dropped like a rock under an avalanche of do-gooder. Vertigo tried to use her abilities and Primal chuckled as if it tickled. Slapping her, he stepped over her unconscious body. Stiletto lunged at his back and her blades bent against his skin. She dodged backwards as he threw a viscous strike at her. Triage began to pour golden light at the broken body of Roughneck. After a minute, he passed out from the pain.

I staggered to my feet with my injured shoulder totally useless. Primal looked around at the pile of battered heroes at his feet and began to stalk towards me. Stiletto beat him to me and began to drag me away. It hurt. Primal took two big steps and leapt into the air. Hurtling over our heads, he landed behind us with a bone shaking crash.

"Not so fast," snarled Primal, "your master isn't here to protect you now."

"No, but I am!" said a voice to our right.

Spinning in place, Primal froze. Not because he wanted too, because he had no choice in the matter, Mediator did. The villain lounged on a broken fruit crate, his immaculate suit gleaming in the slight moonlight.

"Now, Primal, why don't you calm down," grinned the telepath, "there is no reason to be so impolite to our friend, Mr. Tiger."

"You will pay for this," snarled the villain through clenched teeth.

"Maybe I will and maybe I won't," smiled Mediator, "but you need to get some shut eye for now."

As soon as Mediator said the words, Primal collapsed boneless into snoring pile of villain. His lips curled into a sarcastic grimace, Mediator regarded the sleeping brute. Turning away, he walked to me and Stiletto. Stiletto stepped in front of me and took up a defensive stance.

"Calm down, Stil," I said, "he is almost being a good guy today."

"Yeah, it feels sort of weird," grinned the villain, "I may get used to the feeling."

"I owe you another one," I said to him, "at this rate, I am gonna have to keep you on retainer."

"Ha!" laughed Mediator, "Let me go again and we will call it even."

"Deal," I said, "go before Stiletto gets any ideas about being a hero."

"I know what side my bread is buttered on, stupid," she said, "I won't stop him."

"You can't stop me," said Mediator with a knowing smile, "regardless of what you are thinking right now."

"You wanna bet," taunted Stiletto.

"If you think the blade in your boot is going to help you, then pull it out," he replied, "I will make you carve my initials in your own ass with it."

"Stiletto, he can do it," I said, "leave him be."

"Marv...Tiger, your destiny lies to the north," said Mediator as he began to walk away, "but don't forget about what you saw at the Tower. That, also, is your destiny."

"Wait, what is to the north?" I demanded as I limped after him.

Smiling at me, he spoke. "Listen, even though I helped you out, I am still a villain. Helping you too much goes against my nature."

"You are more of a hero than you realize," I returned.

"Maybe once, you were right," he said with a faraway look in his eyes, "but as one lives through the centuries, one drifts more towards evil with each passing year. I have lived on this earth for over 20 centuries. It is too late for me to be a hero but I am working on being neutral."

"Good luck," I said, "you are closer to good than you think."

Nodding, he turned away, took a step, and disappeared. Watching the spot were he had last stood, I shook my head at him and his unfathomable ways. I'll see him again, I thought, I know it.

Stiletto walked up behind me and laced her arm through mine. Supporting me, she lead me over to the pile of unconscious bodies. Leaning me against a phone booth, she went to Triage and knelt down to awaken him. Suddenly, her shoulders fell and she took on a dejected posture.

"He's dead," she said with a thick voice.

"What?" I couldn't believe my ears.

"It looks like his heart burst from the strain," she said.

"Check the others," I ordered. Triage had been a good kid. Wet behind the ears, but brave and fearless. Anyone who knows that using their powers could kill them and still uses those powers for good was a hero in my book.

As she went from hero to hero, a crashing sound came from behind me. Spinning painfully, I turned in time to see Eagle burst through the wall that Primal had thrown him into earlier. His grandfather's costume was torn and dirty. Blood seeped from a wounds that a half ton of falling wall had given him. Rage filled his young eyes.

"Where is he!" roared the boy, his voice sounding like the man he would become.

"He is taken care of," I said to the boy, "help Stil with the others."

The wild look in his eyes subsided and he hurried over to do what he could. As the two of them dressed wounds and provided what meager first aid they could, I heard the sounds of people approaching. Around the corner at the end of the street came a group of about a dozen spandexes. Leading them was a tall man in a blue and white suit covered in snowflakes. Blizzard.

I had heard about him before, he was some big dude in Washington. He was the commander of the East Coast heroes. I knew a woman named Seismic ran the West Coast heroes and Pecos Bill controlled the Midwest.

Blizzard stopped before the scene of battle and signaled for the heroes with him to lend a hand. A couple of them ran forward and began healing the injured. A minute or two after they arrived a brown eyed heroine was plucking the metal shards out of my shoulder and pouring a strange rainbow-slicked liquid into the wounds. Within seconds, the bleeding gashes had grown closed and I felt well enough to stand.

Another hero was examining the body of Triage. I was about to warn him that he was dead when he created a column of light around the hero's still form. Sparkles of starlight spun and danced in the column as wisps of white swirled around the body. Triage's body began twitching and shaking and after a few moments, rolled over and took a breath. The column of light dissipated and the hero who created it moved on to the next person.

"Wait, what did you just do?" I asked of the hero.

"He was only gone for a few minutes. If I get to them soon enough, I can raise the dead," said the hero

Nodding my head, I turned away and looked at Triage. He got lucky, I thought. Flashback didn't get so lucky, nobody had been around to resurrect him. Spying Blizzard looking at me, I walked painfully over to him. He nodded in recognition as he ordered a pair of heroes to patrol around the scene of the battle.

"You're Night Tiger," he said matter-of-factly.

"Guilty as charged," I said, "you gonna arrest me now or later?"

"Heh! I don't think so. If I take action against a hero today, it will be that coward Thunderclap, not you," He replied, "if I had been in your shoes, I would have impaled him on an icicle."

"Well, I didn't happen to have one handy," I replied.

Blizzard laughed. "So, what happened here? I see common street thugs like I have seen all night but I also see some powerhouses catching some shut eye."

"A group of super villains were in control of this area. They attacked us after we wiped out the mob of punks," I said, "we almost didn't make it. They had us on the ropes."

"What happened?" he asked.

"They didn't work together. We did," I explained simply. "and, well, we had help."

"Elaborate."

"A villain named Mediator stopped that guy in his tracks," I said as I pointed towards Primal, "he beat us single handedly."

"Mediator...Do you mean 'Brainpain'?" asked Blizzard.

"Yeah, that's him. He has saved me three times today," I nodded.

"Are you sure we can still call him a villain then?" he asked with humor.

"Yeah, I think it is still safe to say he is," I replied.

While we talked, the heroes with Blizzard had helped my team to their feet. Only Triage was still on the ground, but he was awake and in a daze. Battered and bruised, my group looked like they had been through hell. Twice.

"Listen, you guys look like death warmed over..." began Blizzard.

"Yeah, no kidding," said Triage in a strange far-away voice, "you don't know the half of it."

"Listen, the hotspots in the city are under control. Jinx's team has control of the Aztec district and the Foundry is cleaned up as well. You all go home and rest. We need you fresh tomorrow. There are reports of a Citadel appearing in the middle of Centennial Park to the north."

"But…" I began to object.

"No buts," said Blizzard authoritatively, "go home, rest tonight. Tomorrow, be at City Hall by nine o'clock sharp. That's an order."

"Yes sir," I said.

Nodding at my team, I began to walk back the way we came. Footsteps fell in behind me and I knew the others were following. I didn't speak until we neared Eagle's house.

"Eagle, you fought well tonight," I said, "you honor your grandfather with your bravery. Join us tomorrow. City Hall, 9 o'clock sharp."

"I will," he said as he stood at the edge of his lawn.

I motioned to Gun Control as Eagle walked up the concrete sidewalk to his house. I talked with Gun Control about what I needed him to do tonight and he nodded his agreement. Facing the other heroes, I spoke again.

"Folks, you all proved yourself tonight. All of you. I expect you to be fresh tomorrow," I said, "good night and good luck."

With that, I turned and bounded into the shadows on the nearby alley. Jogging across the next street, I entered the park we had crossed through earlier. Stopping next to the impaled bodies of the city's defenders, I reached into my belt and dropped a medical beacon. Someone would pick them up and give them a proper burial.

Continuing on my home, I saw nobody on the streets. The cities inhabitants, both good and bad, had decided that the fun for this night was over. The sounds of battle that had reverberated throughout the steel and glass canyons had ceased and had been replaced by a thick silence. No cars motored through the streets and no televisions blared out open windows into the night. The city was hunkered down in fear.

My neighborhood was as quiet as a tomb. Moving through the silent streets was unnerving. I drew close to my apartment building and walked up the steps to the heavy glass doors. I pushed them open and saw the fat guy standing behind the counter with an odd look on his face. His frozen expression set me on edge and the gun in his hand sent me over it. Dodging to the left, the fat man didn't react. Drawing close to his still form, I could see that he was alive but paralyzed. Noticing a small dart in his arm, I pulled it out and sniffed the tip. Poison.

I couldn't tell what kind but it smelled like it wasn't fatal. I pried the shotgun from his hands and gently moved him into a nearby chair. I rubbed his arms and legs, trying to get his blood flowing and moving the poison out of his system. After a few minutes, he began to move sluggishly. A few more minutes and he was trying to speak.

"Grrrooupp offff wiimmen…" he drawled with effort.

"A group of women did this to you?" I asked

He nodded, "Toook giirlll."

"They took a girl…" I pondered.

And then it hit me. They didn't take a girl…They took my girl. Leaving the fat guy, I burst through the stairwell door and ran up the steps. I took them four at a time, literally leaping and bounding upwards. I hit the door to my floor like a battering ram and it's old hinges shattered with the impact.

The door to my apartment was broken and lay in shards on my floor. My apartment was ransacked. Furniture smashed, television destroyed, and my spare costume had been ripped to shreds. A note lay on the ruins of my table. Grabbing it up, I read aloud the two words on the paper.

"Centennial Park."

A Walk in the Park

"This is gonna be a walk in the park."
—Silent Scream, villain

There had been a reason that I kept to myself. The punks that I fought each day were dangerous and crazy. There was no telling what they might do. My whole life as a hero in this city and I never had a partner, never had a real friend. I never had a girlfriend. It was just too dangerous for them. And even more so for me.

Because of the way my mother passed and how that left me, I was not good at dealing with the loss of loved ones. So, I simply refused to love any one. Hell, I had even made it a rule. Don't get involved, I said, don't get too close. Fat lot of good that did me.

A pretty lady batted her brown eyes at me and my much vaunted rule flew right out the window. A simple smile and she had me. A quick kiss kept me. What was wrong with me? I had barely begun to know this woman and I was acting like a schoolboy. Hell, schoolboys have more style.

The shadows hid me as I ran down a dirty alleyway. Making a right at the opening, I jogged to the corner. Looking around, I saw the building I was looking for. It was a small, two story brick house nestled between a couple of squat apartment buildings. A dingy wooden door gave a heavy sound when I knocked. A silver panel swung open beside the door. A small screen displayed the face of the man I was here to see.

"Take off the spandex for the night?" I asked Gun Control.

"Yeah, it inhibits me too much when I am working," he explained, "come on in."

The wood door swung open soundlessly. I stepped into a room that in no way resembled the exterior of the house. Silver, machined-metal walls were crowded with numerous devices and workstations. Long tracks of fluorescent lighting gave a cold, unnatural glow to the room. Different kinds of partitions separated the space but for the most part the entire floor was one big mad science laboratory. Lightning arced from slender rods and different contraptions beeped and booped sonnets for the nerds in all of us. I have to admit, I was impressed.

The man I knew as Gun Control was puttering about near a table covered in microscopes and trays of tiny instruments. Without his protective armor, he was nothing remarkable. A slender man in his early thirties, he looked more like a computer programmer than a super hero. Sharp eyes were bordered by dark circles and fatigue lines became visible as his mask of concentration slipped. Glancing up from his fancy microscope, he nodded to me wearily.

"Come here," he said, "I have a present for you."

"Great! I love presents!" I replied as I walked towards him.

Pulling a stool beside the table, he motioned me in it. I looked around the table as he grabbed up a small hypodermic needle. Aside from a couple of different microscopes, there were also several trays with assorted unrecognizable instruments. The tray he took the needle from also contained a couple of ampoules with a blue substance inside them. He took one of the vials and screwed it into the needle gun.

"I thought about what you asked me to do tonight and I decided that an armored suit was not what you needed," he explained as he rolled up my sleeve, "instead, I created a different solution to your problem."

Ramming the needle gun against my arm, he depressed the trigger. Pain slammed into my arm and a numbing sensation arced through my entire left side. He stepped away quickly as I staggered off the stool. I tried to grab him with my right arm and pay him back for poisoning me but the numb feeling spread and I collapsed onto the cool metal floor. The last thing I remember before I passed out was Gun Control turning and walking away from me. The bastard.

I awoke to a techno-cacophony. The machines I noticed in the room had all been turned on and commanded to drive me crazy with a thousand different electronic noises. I was stretched out on a metal examining table. Sturdy metallic clamps pinned me around every conceivable joint and a few that weren't conceivable. My entire body was immobilized.

Gun Control stepped into my field of vision and leaned down to carefully study my face. Nodding to himself, he turned and stepped out of my sight. I heard him take a few steps and sit down in a chair with a slightly squeaky spring. I then heard him begin to clack away on a keyboard. I tried to shift myself on the uncomfortable table and was greeted with no movement and a much louder clanging in my ears from the machines.

"Awake at last, I see," said Gun Control as I heard him stand.

"Yeah," I replied through clenched jaws, "I'm awake alright."

"How do you feel?" he asked as he stepped back into sight.

"Like shit," I replied, "after all, you did just poison me. How did you think I would feel"

"Poison you?" he stammered, "Are you crazy?"

He stepped out of sight again and this time I heard him slam his hand against some sort of button. The clamor immediately stopped and my restraints let go with a clunk. Sitting up on the table, I glared at him as I rubbed my sore arms.

"No, I'm not crazy," I replied angrily, "if that wasn't poison, then what was it?"

"It was a present. Follow me and I will show you," said Gun Control with a grin on his face.

Walking away from the desk he was leaning against, he sauntered over to a partitioned area. Punching a set of numbers into the keypad beside the door, he turned back to me and gestured me over. The door slid open with a hiss and a blue light winked on inside the small room.

"Inside," he said, "you have to trust me."

"I am not big on trusting others," I said.

"Give it a shot. You may be surprised," he countered.

Gritting my teeth, I stalked past him into the room. Inside, there were several machines I did not recognize. Most seemed like computers for recording information while others seemed like a madman designed a nautilus.

Gun Control led me over to one of the medieval torture devices and made me sit down on it. I placed my hands and feet in what appeared to be the appropriate places as he began to turn on a multitude of chattering machines.

"You are sitting in a device I designed to determine your speed, strength, agility, and reflexes," he explained proudly.

"Sounds fancy," I replied sarcastically.

"It is," he said as he flipped a switch, "I got the idea from a taffy puller."

My eyes widened in shock as the machine began to try to twist and contort my body into a super pretzel. Struggling against the machine's efforts I was able to slow it's movements to a halt. A high pitched whine began to sound and the machine began to jitter and smoke. Gun Control leapt from the console he was studying and slammed his hand against a big red button on the side of the device I was strapped to. Immediately the machine stopped trying to bend me like Stretch Armstrong. Gun Control hurried to release me from the straps that held me in the machine.

"They work!" he said with glee as he freed me, "And they work better than I thought they would!"

"Who are they and how do they work?" I demanded.

"Nanotechnology," he explained as he turned back to his console, "tiny, simple robots that live inside your body and perform different functions. They are the next logical step in medicine and weaponry. I injected nanotech of my own design into you."

"What do these robots do inside me?" I asked warily. I wasn't so sure about what I was getting in to.

"They increased your strength, speed, agility, and reflexes nearly ten fold. In fact, they may have also increased your senses, regeneration, and toughness," he positively danced as he studied his readouts, "congratulations on your new superpowers, Night Tiger."

"Super powers?" I said with disbelief.

"Yep," he said, "coupled with your already considerable martial arts talent, the nanotech will make you a one man wrecking crew."

"I kinda like the sound of that," I said warily, "but what are the side effects of this nanny-tech stuff."

"Nanotech. And there aren't any side effects to my knowledge," he answered, "except for really surprising any of your enemies when you meet up with them again, that is."

I grinned at him. He was right, I did like his present to me. Actually, now that I think about it, it was the best present I had ever gotten. Except for those legos I got when I was six. I loved my legos.

We walked out of the small room together. Nodding my thanks at him, I turned to leave. He paused as I walked away but spoke as I neared the door. His nervousness was evident in his tone.

"You are going to the park, aren't you?" he asked.

"Yeah. I have business there tonight," I answered without turning to face him, "personal business."

"Don't you need backup?" he said in disbelief.

"Not now, thanks to you," I answered as I opened the door into the dark night, "not anymore."

The door slammed behind me as I leapt into the beckoning shadows. The night concealed my newfound abilities, even from me. But even without ample light, I was able to notice a remarkable difference in my usual movements. My bound from Gun Control's front door carried nearly across the street. My first few strides ate up the distance to the corner as if I were the only thing in the world moving at normal speed. The darkened windows and recessed doorways flitted past my peripheral vision like a slide show on fast forward. Litter danced in each step of my wake as if I were Hermes himself. Wind whistled in my ears as I whipped to my left into the dark alleyway I had emerged from earlier. Gathering my strength, I soared upwards with a leap. Grabbing the railing of the fire escape above, I vaulted over and raced up the stairwell.

Reaching the roof, I sprinted across the large area of gravel. I leapt upon the ledge when I reached it and surveyed the distance to the next building. A large alleyway separated the old apartment building I was on and the newer brownstone across the way. Gathering my strength, I prepared to make a twenty foot leap. When I left my feet, I quickly realized that I had made a major mistake. My new powers had increased my leaping ability nearly tenfold. I kept going and going and going…did I mention I kept going?

I easily cleared the brownstone and the next building before I had even reached the halfway point. On my descent, I realized that I was about to land in a rather disgusting looking dumpster. Rotten garbage scattered when I impacted, some of the smaller pieces reached nearly 20 feet in height before falling to the dirty pavement. The force I carried was so strong that the walls of the dumpster bowed outward slightly when I landed. This was going to take some getting used to.

Extracting myself from my rather smelly landing, I shook my head as I brushed the stinking garbage off my uniform. Gun Control's present was much more complicated than it seemed at first. Looking back at the demolished dumpster, I figured that it would be safer if I just jogged the rest of the way to the park. No reason to put the garbage companies out of business just to save a few minutes of travel time, I supposed.

I was only about half an hour's jog from the park at my usual speed. I covered the distance in under eight minutes. The soles of my boots were as soft as taffy and very warm to the touch when I slid to a halt within sight of Centennial Park. I guess I should sign up for the marathon next month. A super hero has to eat, after all.

At normal times, Centennial Park could be a very dangerous place. Groups of mutated Vagabonds controlled most of it after the sun goes down. While the sun was up, the bums only appeared to control some of the less traveled walkways. However, appearances could be deceiving. I was ready for the park as I knew it, not as it actually was.

The twelve foot tall brick wall separating the island of nature from it's ugly steel and concrete stepsister had changed. It was now over twenty feet tall and sloped outwards at the top. Black spikes of warped and twisted bone crowned the wall and the bricks of the wall were blood red and grotesquely pitted and marred. The trees that were visible over the hellish structure twisted and swayed in a macabre dance. Dark limbs grabbed for the scant moonlight, drinking the sickly illumination. What little light that filtered through the canopy was the color of pale death and the texture of a burial shroud. Chill winds carried a dark stench as they whistled through the shadowy mass of trees. Strange cries fell from the dark maze of branches, unworldly sounds of despair and weeping sorrow. Movement could be glimpsed out of the corner of the eye. Skittering and slithering through the treetops, warped beings stayed just out of the diffuse glow of the moon. Just what I needed, a walk in the park.

Hugging the shadows, I quickly picked my way down the block. The nearest entrance to the park was in sight when I ducked into a nearby doorway. Hunkered in the deep pools of night, I peered intently at the entrance. The stone columns that normally marked the end of the wall had been replaced by black obsidian spires that crookedly strained for the blanket of night. Wrought iron gates had been warped and twisted into metal teeth that opened beckoningly to me. The sidewalk had taken on a red hue that resembled nothing more than a deep pool of fresh blood. Wails of agony sounded between my ears with each clang of the swinging gates. What was I thinking?

Sure, I had gone toe to toe with a few bad dudes in my day and I had been in a few rough spots. I had been caught in gang battles and alien invasions. I had stood side by side with other heroes to turn back an army of marauding villains. But none of that mattered now, this was something much worse.

It was as if the park itself was a hungry beast waiting for me to walk into it's mouth. Gazing at the entranceway, I could feel a tugging sensation deep within my belly. Faint melodies of suffering and pain filtered into my ears. Shadows danced a marionette's waltz just inside the depths of the park. I was about to take my first step when a chorus of bloodcurdling screams rose up from the depths of the dark and twisted forest.

I realized at that moment that I had to make a choice. Tonight, I had to decide if I was going into the park as a hero or as Michelle's protector. I knew the second I heard those screams that I would be faced with the choice of saving someone or remaining hidden. And that was no choice at all, tonight I was off the clock. Tonight was for me.

Darting across the street, I placed my back against the black spire. Peering around the corner, my eyes could not pierce the gloom. Sliding across the cold iron bars, I gripped the gate and swung it open with a squeal that sounded like the cries of hell itself. Wincing at the noise, I plunged into the darkness.

My first step in the shadow was an eternity wrapped up in a moment. The dark grabbed me and held me close to it's vile bosom. My skin crawled with the squirming of maggots. Smells I cannot to this day identify filled my nostrils. Sights best unseen capered in my vision. The taste of a thousand rotting corpses coated my tongue. Voices shattered my ears with wails, none more loud than my own. Then something changed.

The sounds and sights fell away, the tastes and smells fled. I felt cold. Just cold, not pain or fear or disgust. The feeling reminded me of the way Mediator shut down my senses. Maybe Gun Control's robots helped out more than just my physical abilities. The shadows receded into almost normal shapes and for the first time I was able to actually see Centennial Park. It was a nightmare made real. Twisted trees lined dark pathways into the heart of a dead forest. Several bodies were suspended from the canopy of limbs, desecrated in unspeakable ways. Blood had pooled at the feet of the poor tortured souls. Drawing near one of the bodies, I could not believe what I saw.

It was one of the Vagabonds. Somebody had nailed him to the trunk of a warped oak tree. His dirty shirt had been ripped to shreds and hung in tattered strips from his torso. His chest had been carved upon. Runic symbols created by a madman stretched across the man's belly, creating a mural of insanity on his body. His throat had been torn out savagely, showing ragged edges of skin bled white. A look of supreme terror was frozen upon his still face.

Vagabonds were homeless people who had been exposed to some of the toxic sludge that had been dumped in some of the city's waterways. All had developed grotesque physical mutations but some had acquired different powers. They had basically taken over Centennial Park but were more or less harmless. Unless you didn't bring any spare change with you.

Regardless of their nuisance level and appearance, nobody deserved to be mutilated and tortured to death. Swallowing my anger, I stalked down the dark path ignoring the other shapes staked to the tree trunks. I had gone about two hundred feet it seemed before my senses sharpened with a vengeance. I could hear sawing breath and smell perspiration laced with fear. A group of people were hurrying down the path towards the exit. And I was standing between them and the exit. Looking around, I dodged off the path and into a small copse of trees. Extending my claws, I speared them into a thick trunk and pulled myself up. Grabbing a branch, I perched on it about fifteen feet above the path.

Scurrying down the path came a small group of Vagabonds lead by two in particular. I recognized them. On the left was a big bruiser with massive facial scars called Panhandle and on the right was a dirty, slouched man called Sterno. I had busted them years ago for a simple extortion racket they had set up. Now, they seemed to be some sort of bigwigs with the bums. Talk about moving up in the world.

"Are they still behind us?" asked Sterno in a reedy whisper.

"I haven't heard them in a few minutes," answered Panhandle.

"The exit is this way?" asked Sterno, "You're sure?"

"Yeah. It's a couple of hundred yards up the path to the Park street exit," nodded Panhandle.

Turning away, the bigger bum began to move down the path. Sterno watched for a split second and then trailed after. The others quickly followed in line. They got about four steps.

One of the nameless Vagabonds suddenly screamed and everyone froze at the sound. Catching myself, I turned to the man and saw him being slaughtered by a seven foot tall demon. Similar in appearance to the demon lord I had seen, this one did not exude the raw power that Agzamoth did. Nonetheless, the demon was still a formidable creature. Massive muscles strained to burst as the creature literally ripped the poor Vagabond in half. Black claws sliced skin like a shark's fin cutting through water. Long fangs bit deeply into warm flesh.

The scream that paralyzed the Vagabonds served to spell their doom as well. Crashing out of the forest at the apex of the wail came a wave of small monstrosities that swarmed over the men. Panhandle crushed half a dozen before a solid wall of mind numbing creatures crashed into him and Sterno incinerated a few before they sank their black claws into him. Striding through the throng of imps came a demon to be reckoned with. Towering nearly ten feet in height, small stubby wings were just beginning to appear on it's back. Snatching up a smoking ruin of sniveling imp, the demon ripped it's head off in a single bite. Gulping in satisfaction the larger demon walked through devouring injured beings with reckless abandon. Each death increasing it's power, it's strength. Bending down, the large demon grabbed Panhandle and held him aloft like a man holds a kitten. Shaking the sobbing bum, the demon glared at the mass of hellish creatures.

"Despicable beings! These are not who we are looking for," snarled the monster, "these are nothing more than meat."

Ramming Panhandle against the bole of a tree, the demon ripped a jagged piece of wood from the branches. Holding his quarry's hands up, the demon slowly pushed the jagged stake through flesh. Shivering with the pleasure of Panhandle's suffering, the demon paused before it ripped his shirt aside and began to slash runes into the man's chest. Fey energies gathered and the Vagabond's eyes widened in unspeakable pain as his soul was ripped from his body. Screaming triumph at the feast of energy, the demon bent his head and ripped Panhandle's throat out. Blood and meat fell from the demon's lips as he addressed his minions.

"Find the one we are searching for or face my wrath," snarled the monster, "bring me the striped one. Bring me the Night Tiger or die."

Striding up the path, the large demon lead the other creatures towards the entrance. Looking down at the destruction and death left in their wake, I wondered what the hell I had gotten myself into. Trying to ignore the carnage, I slipped down the tree and set my feet on the path. The less time I spent thinking about this nightmare, the better.

Time passed, quickly or slowly I could not tell, and soon I was nearing the center of the park. This was where the Citadel had supposedly appeared. I had stayed off the path as much as I could without getting too deep into the trees. That would no longer be an option. The path ahead widened to the edge of the treeline, forming a ragged circle. I would be forced to step into the pool of sickly moonlight that covered the path to proceed. The park was unnaturally quiet. No wind rustled the dry leaves, no small animals crept through the grass. Screw it.

Stepping into the moonlight, I confidently strode into the clearing. No reason to beat around the bush, in more ways than one. If something was waiting to grab me, I might as well give them the chance. So near to my goal, I decided to throw caution to the wind.

My first strides into the clearing enabled me to get my first glimpse of the Citadel. No wonder rumors about it were spreading around the city. It towered over the treetops like a gleaming white finger pointing to Heaven. A soft golden glow surrounded it and gently filled the night sky with light. It was breathtaking but I shook off my stupor and continued down the path.

Matching me step for step came a man from the other side of the clearing. He was immaculately dressed in a well made business suit. In his hand was an expensive leather briefcase. He mirrored my movements until we stood face to face in the center of the clearing. He held his briefcase in front of himself in two hands, almost like a shield.

"Welcome, Mr. Tiger," he said in flat tones, "you have been expected."

"Well, you're not quite what I expected," I shot back, "I figured you would be one of those demons."

"No, I'm much worse," he said with a slight smile, "I'm a lawyer. I represent certain parties that would like to have a word with you."

"You're right, I would have preferred demons," I smirked.

"You may get your wish. There are dozens of them laying in wait between here and the Citadel. You can risk your chances with them and their not-so-tender ways or you can surrender to me and I can escort you through them," he explained, "it's your choice."

"The lady or the tiger?" I said.

"Quite so. Even more so in this case than usual, if you will forgive the irony," he answered.

"And what would happen if I decided to simply knock your head off and take my chances with the demons?" I grinned savagely.

"You wouldn't make it three steps," he replied.

He was wrong. I made it five steps. The look of surprise on the lawyer's face was worth the pummeling I received. I open hand slapped him and he dropped like a rock. I sprinted a few steps before shapes came hurtling out of the trees towards me. I never had a chance. Small beings tripped my feet up as larger, more man-sized creatures tackled me from both sides. Savagely, I attempted to struggle as they tore into me with in a frenzy. Within seconds, I was bleeding from dozens of small wounds and the Kevlar plates in my costume had been ripped out and cast aside. Pinning my arms and legs, my attackers held me aloft as the larger demon I had seen earlier bounded into the moonlight. Pausing at the unconscious body of the lawyer, the monstrosity smiled in such a way as to send shivers of revulsion down my spine. Impaling the man on one of his long talons caused the lawyer's eyes to snap open and a piteous wail escaped his lips. The demon lifted the man over his head and held him as he wriggled and squirmed in agony. Laughing, the demon tossed the lawyer aside with his entrails falling behind him like a child with a captured junebug on a string. Catching my eye, the demon smiled again and this time was worse than the last because he meant it.

"He is the one. The mistress will be pleased," smiled the demon as he walked towards me.

Stopping before me, the monster leaned down and peered intently at my face. Making eye contact, the demon stared at me with horrible eyes colored with promises of suffering. I stared back with eyes nearly bored to tears. I couldn't help myself, I knew that this one was nothing more than a servant. He would not be the one I would have to worry about. A slight smile played itself out on the corners of my mouth. Blossoming into an insolent grin as the demon's eyes widened in shock, I spit in it's face. The demon was frozen with shock that an insignificant human would dare to insult him.

"I've seen demons before. You're not that impressive, slave," I smirked.

Roaring in anger, the demon lashed out and slammed a backhand into my face. My head snapped sideways and the monsters holding me fell into a pile from the force of the blow. I kept my eyes closed as I heard the demon approach. His blow had barely even registered. Gun Control's robots had made me strong enough to take whatever these lesser monsters had to throw at me. But there was no reason for them to know that. At least for right now...

The demon snorted near my face. Fetid breath washed over me like swimming in the wake of a garbage scow. Grabbing my shredded costume, the demon hauled me up and shook me. I continued to play 'possum as it snorted again and tossed me over it's broad shoulders. I heard the clatter of clawed feet as the throng of smaller demons scurried away from my captor. It was taking me into the Citadel. Who woulda thought that my Trojan horse would be a ten foot tall demon with an inferiority complex.

I felt the demon carry me up a short flight of stairs and then heard his footsteps reverberating inside a large chamber. Cracking my eyes open, I could see the demon's legs walking across a floor of onyx flecked with gold. It's snakelike tail whipped and twitched from underneath the short metal skirt the monster wore. It stopped walking and I heard it push a door open. Seconds later, I was thrown upon the cold stone floor. I kept my eyes closed as I felt the monster staring at me. Then I heard the door slam and the demon walk away.

I opened my eyes. I was on the floor of a large circular room. Shiny sets of chains hung from stone fixtures in the round walls. The room had a sort of new car smell but in this case it was more of a new prison smell. The door of the room had a small window covered by a set of five inch thick metal bars. The floor, walls, and ceiling were all made of the same onyx with gold flecks. The door was stout oak with iron bands. Enough to keep a man locked up for a long time. Lucky for me, I was more than a simple man now.

Crossing over to the door, I studied it closely. After a moment of inspection, I grabbed the handle with one hand and a bar with the other and simply ripped the door off it's frame. Stepping through, I set the door carefully back in place. It would appear normal until someone got close to it. Looking around, I got my first view of the Citadel.

Wow. My jaw dropped at the beauty of the room I was standing in. The onyx floor competed with rose quartz columns that literally bled gorgeous crimson light. Tapestries of the finest quality tastefully covered flat expanses of the walls. A roof of crystallized amber floated over my head. Alcoves contained exquisite statues of the purest marble. Arched entrances were visible around the room, all surrounded by tropical flowers in bloom. Fine furniture from what appeared to be Roman origins completed the room. I was stunned. It may have been the most wonderful place I had ever been. But it needed a pool table.

Focusing, I was able to pick up the smell of the demon who brought me in. He had taken the second door on the left. I figured he would go report to his boss and following him would be a good idea. My only concern was Michelle and the best place to start would be with whoever was behind all this. My path chosen, I set off after the demon.

The hallways I traveled were as stunning as the room I had left. I quickly realized that all the perfection and beauty began to run together, making it hard to focus on where I was going and where I had been. My nose lead me, without it I would have been lost after the first turn. Even with his stench showing me the way, I still had doubts after passing what appeared to be the same statue for the third time. But I should have known to trust my nose, it hadn't let me down and it didn't this time either.

I turned a corner with the stink of the demon filling my nostrils and nearly ran into a pair of demons standing guard. Luckily, they were turned away and didn't see me dart back around the edge of the wall. My mind tried to make some sense from what I had seen in the scant moment I had faced through the doorway.

The two demons had been standing on either side of a large archway. They had been staring into the room beyond. What I could glimpse of the room, it had been filled with demons and humans sitting in a stadium. Peeking back around the corner, the demons were still staring into the arena room. Stepping back, I grabbed a small marble statue. Walking around the corner, I cracked the demon on my left on the back of his head. The other turned at the noise as the one I hit dropped like a stone. I leaned my head to the side and grinned wide at the monster looking at me with a puzzled expression. My snap kick rocked his head backwards and my punch slammed him against the wall. Two puddles of sleeping demon rested on either side of me as I looked in to see what was so important. Michelle, that's what.

Suspended from chains connected to a crooked black spire, Michelle had been dressed in a red and white dominatrix outfit. Capering in the sands twenty feet below her were a horde of small imps. Occasionally, one would leap upwards and claw at the spire. Each leap brought the imps closer and closer to Michelle. The stands around the arena floor were packed with men and women and otherworldly monsters. At one end of the arena, a raised platform held a small throne with a beautiful woman sitting in it. Surrounding her were women dressed in the same outfit Michelle was wearing. Each woman was carrying a different weapon, from swords, to whips, to one woman carrying a crossbow. The lady in the throne was very familiar. Angel.

It figured. Every time I turned around, one of these Shadow Chamber goombahs showed up to start some trouble for me. Well, this time Angel had gone too far. This time she had made it personal. And she was going to pay for it.

"I enjoy the view from here as well," said a evil voice behind me.

Great. If I keep getting snuck up on, I was going to have to turn in my junior ninja badge. Of course, this time I might get a pass. The thing that snuck up on me was a supernatural creature. Ehh, who was I kidding? I just wasn't paying attention and something got the drop on me. Again.

"Where is your friend?" asked the demon as I turned to face him.

"Friend?" I asked as I tried to count the number of demons in the hallway behind me. I stopped trying when I reached twenty.

"The young one," said the demon with an evil grimace, "the young boy who ripped the door open and freed you. The strong one."

"I sent him away," I lied, "he's too young for this."

"One is never too young for the sights we can show," said the demon while licking what passed for it's lips, "in fact, the younger the better."

"And I would've thought a big bad demon like you would want more of a challenge than a child," I taunted, "but then again, I told you that you weren't that impressive. It makes perfect sense."

The demon smiled even wider. He wasn't going to be goaded this time. He wanted me awake for what was to come. He gestured with a muscular arm and the horde with him surrounded me and lead me into the arena. I allowed myself to be swept along. After all, I was headed into the arena one way or another. Might as well do it with some dignity.

The crowd hushed it's raucous cheering when me and my demon entourage entered the arena. After a second's pause, hushed murmurs began to ripple through the throng of beings. I could see Angel's smirk from half an arena away as she leaned forward to scrutinize me. She gestured to one of her attending women and spoke behind a hand to her. Within seconds, Angel sat back on her throne and six of her guards hustled from the stage in my direction. Six hot women in lingerie hustling, that's a great visual.

The women intersected the group that held me captive quickly. The small demons in the front snarled and hissed at the women and the women sniffed disdainfully back at them. The biggest demon stepped behind me and grabbed my shoulder in one clawed hand.

"Stand aside, meat. I go to present my prize to the mistress," growled the demon.

"The mistress thanks you for your prize. He is to be given to us and taken to the arena floor," smiled one of the women, "we have something special in mind for him."

Hissing in anger, the demon let go of my shoulder and stepped back. When he did, the other demons followed his lead and quickly backed away from the six women. Stepping around me, the women replaced the demons as my captors. With weapons drawn they escorted me down into the arena and across the warm sand.

Showdown in the Sand

"When I played in the sandbox, the cat kept covering me up."
—Rodney Dangerfield, comedian

Michelle hung with her head down, her dark hair covered her face. The chains holding her cut deeply into her arms and small trickles of blood were evident on her wrists. As we neared the spire, she raised her head weakly and we locked eyes. Tracks of tears raced down her face and stress lines marred her perfect skin. We kept eye contact as the women shackled my arms and legs and hauled me up beside her. Summoning up all my courage, I looked into her fearful eyes as the women walked away. I had to say something to ease her fear, I had to say something memorable.

"I love your outfit."

She grinned at me and that was all the thanks I needed. Her breath hitched in her throat as she tried to say something to me. Sobs began to wrack her body as she struggled with what she was about to say.

"Marvin...I'm sorry," she began, "I'm sorry about all this. I was supposed to get close to you somehow and then murder you. But you were so kind to me and didn't ask for anything from me. You were the first person to ever do that. I've done a lot of jobs and you were the first one that I actually cared about..."

Just as I was about to interrupt her apology, Angel beat me to it. Speaking into a microphone, her voice cut through the chatter in the arena. When she began speaking both Michelle and I turned to stare at her.

"Tonight, we are faced with a momentous occasion. Not only do we get to execute a traitor but we also get to sacrifice the chosen one," boomed Angel's voice, terrible and bright, "tonight, Azgamoth's reign will be assured and we all shall be placed high in his glory!"

I wasn't sure which part of that statement hit me harder. The chosen one part or the traitor part? Looking sidelong at Michelle, I knew. I knew that she was a part of this group and had betrayed my trust and love. I also knew that she had betrayed this group out of trust and love for me. When she raised her stricken face towards me, I forgave her in an instant.

"Don't sweat it," I whispered across to her, "it'll be okay. These things tend to work out for me"

"How can you say that?" she asked as Angel continued to rant and rave, "We are about to get slaughtered by a bunch of demons and the Succubae. I was a Succubus, they are no joke."

"Succubus, huh? I like the sound of that," I said rakishly, "you'll have to show me after this is all over."

"I can but it would kill you," she grinned back grimly.

"Sounds like fun!" I said.

As we talked, Angel wrapped up her monologue and evil sounding trumpets blew a loud discordant note. Metal gates squealed open and a mob of imps join the small group huddled behind the spire. Now, fifty something imps squirmed in a pile at our feet. For all the tension in the room, I still could not help but laugh at the imps. They were like little evil midgets in a rugby scrum. They were far from fear inspiring.

Then the horns sounded again and a small door opened under Angel's platform. Two of the Succubae walked out flanking the large demon. They quickly marched across the sand and stopped before us. The women began weaving weird patterns in the air with their hands and humming an odd melody. The demon raised his hands upwards and began howling. Above the three, a glowing ball of energy began to form. After a few seconds, the ball had grown to nearly ten feet in diameter. Finishing his howl at the same time that the women completed their part of the spell, the demon was in perfect position to catch the ball of energy. Holding the glowing ball aloft, the demon grinned up at me.

"Such lessons to teach you, human. And so little time!" laughed the monster as it threw the ball of energy at the squirming mass of imps.

The three turned and walked away as the ball struck the imps. Immediately, the ball melted into the mass of creatures and began to glow even brighter. The glow began to spiral and swirl and the features of the imps that I could still see began to stretch and flow into a weird mass. Ten seconds passed before the intensity of the spinning glow became so powerful that everyone had to look away. Suddenly, the glow exploded in a brilliant flash of light, a loud bang, and the horrible stench of the grave.

The massive dog pile of imps had become a seething and rolling blob of flesh. As I watched in horror, the mass began to twist and convulse. I looked over at Michelle as the disgusting blob formed a weird orifice. The look of near insanity in her eyes was enough to spur me into movement.

Straining against my bonds, I quickly shattered the iron chains holding me. Two quick jabs with a steel hard finger crushed the locks on my manacles. Ramming my fingertips into the spire, I created a handle for myself from sheer force. Seconds later, I had freed Michelle and began to climb down the black rock. All in all, I had freed both of us in under twenty seconds. Way too slow.

While I had been struggling against my own chains, the blob had started hiccupping in a most disturbing way. By the time I had crushed my manacles, a slimy torso was emerging from the depths of the mass. By the time Michelle was in my arms, a massive monstrosity slouched waiting for me at the base.

It stood nearly 8 feet in height and probably weighed around 600 pounds. Blood and ichor dripped from its deformed body. A massive club-like arm was contrasted by a viciously clawed hand on the other side. A face even a mother couldn't love adorned a corpulent body. I wasn't worried. I've had blind dates once who looked worse.

As I neared its reach, it darted forward with surprising speed. Its clawed hand lashed out and slashed into the spire where I had hung suspended microseconds before. As it began its charge, I had pushed off and somersaulted over its head. Placing Michelle on the warm sand,

I spun to face the monster just as it charged me again. Taking a step, I leapt at the creature and extended my claws in mid-air. I slashed into its chest at the same time that its clubbed arm slammed into my side. Even with my enhanced abilities, I felt the impact. Bouncing on the sand, I rolled to my feet as the monster's clawed hand slashed through the air beside me. Ramming one of my claws into the monster's left eye gave me a second to spin away and put some distance between us. The creature howled in pain and anger for a second and then turned on me like an enraged bear. Rushing at me in berserker mode, the creature flailed madly.

Luckily for me, the first shot that landed was from the club arm and not the clawed one. The impact sent me flying into the stone spire. I shot a look at Michelle and saw her glancing at the door under the platform. As I attempted to see what interested her over there, the monster's clawed hand filled my vision. Ducking, I was able to avoid its attack. Stepping to its side as it tried to recover, I grabbed a link of chain off the ground. Wrapping the chain around the creature's neck, I leapt on its shoulders and placed my knee on the back of its head. Pulling with all my might, I began to choke the savage creature. It flailed and thrashed and generally put on a good showing but the question was never in doubt. Within a few seconds, the creature was slowing and began to stumble. Quickly, it burned through its remaining oxygen and slumped to the sand unconscious.

As I started to crawl off the stinking wretch, I saw Michelle backing towards me. A cracking sound appeared at the same time that sand flew upwards on her right side. She dodged to her left and I saw the two women and the demon advancing on us. One demon and one woman was fair. Two women and one demon wasn't. Jerking the length of chain free, I ripped it in half and threw both sections one right after the other. The first length of chain sped towards the woman armed with the whip and she dodged to the left. The second length of chain hit her full in the face and dropped her like a bad habit. Whew! I guessed right.

Michelle shot a look back at me and her gratitude was evident in her face. I was scoring some major brownie points tonight. As the whip lady went down, the other women leapt at Michelle swinging a tai chi

136

sword. Michelle dodged her and used the opening to sprint away from her attacker. I stepped off the body of the monster completely and grinned at the advancing demon.

"Your little friends cannot help you now, human," taunted the demon as it regarded it's black talons, "it is just you and I and I have been hungry for a challenge. So try to make this interesting."

It leapt at me, its short wings giving its jump more loft. It landed with a thud as I rolled out of it's path. A snakelike tail swept out and knocked my legs out from under me. The demon chuckled as it slowly circled me. I carefully rose to my feet and grinned back into the demon's vile face.

"My friends didn't come tonight. I don't need them to take the likes of you on," I said, "I was the one who destroyed that door. I'm the new, improved Night Tiger."

The demon began to chuckle at my statement in the same instance that I rushed at its throat. To its credit, it was able to get its hands up and catch mine before I could close them around his neck. Locked up, we strained and struggled against each other. His tail darted in and landed several blows before trying to worm its way around my neck. I bit down hard on the tail when it got near to my mouth and a spray of acidic blood scorched my tongue. The demon screamed in pain and rage and lost its concentration for only a second. But that was a second too long.

Letting go of its hand with my right, I yanked the demon towards me with my left. As the demon stumbled forward, I lashed out with my right hand. As my strike neared the demon, I extended my claws. My swipe ripped the demon's neck open and a sad gurgle came from it's mouth. It stumbled around for a moment then collapsed onto the brackish pool of blood and sand at its feet.

Looking up from the demon's dying breath, I saw Michelle and the woman locked in mortal combat. The woman's sword lay to the side, it's blade bent and useless. Michelle bled from a few cuts across her stomach and a serious wound on her leg. Her attacker suddenly forced Michelle to the sand and seemed to have the upper hand as I tried to run through all the molasses that had suddenly grabbed my feet. The world slowed even more as Michelle grabbed the woman's hair and pulled her into a long passionate kiss. This is the part where I grin at you and raise my eyebrows!

Suddenly the woman's back arched and she scrambled upright with a wheezing scream on her lips. She stumbled around the arena floor with her hands at her throat, a look of panic and confusion on her face. Her eyes were wide as she fell to the sand near me. I grabbed her shoulder and turned her over. Her lips had turned blue, her fingertips had begun to bled and her eyes had started to melt in their sockets. Looking up, I caught Michelle's eye as she watched the woman die.

"That was some kiss," I said somberly.

"You have no idea," she replied from a thousand miles away, "see how this one compares."

She grabbed me and pressed her lips against mine. At first I resisted, thinking I was in store for melting eyeballs but when no pain came I relaxed and enjoyed it. The hectic atmosphere of the arena stopped like an insect trapped in amber. The sounds of a roaring crowd froze mid-note. The fear and pain and stress fell away like a bad dream in the morning light. Then we broke contact, staring at each other breathlessly.

The screaming of the crowd finally kicked back in around us and the world tripped back into normal speed. Angel was standing on her platform, her arms upraised and a look of fury on her face. Stalking onto the sands, were dozens of demons and hundreds of imps. Following in their wake were the Succubae leading small hordes of supplicants. This was gonna hurt…a lot.

"I'm sorry," whispered Michelle, never taking her eyes off the advancing horde, "I was supposed to kill you and instead I loved you and killed us both. I'm so sorry."

"It's okay darling. This is a pretty good death," I smiled sadly, "Well, as far as deaths go anyway."

She grinned back at me and turned to face her doom. I wanted nothing more than to reach out and hold her when the end came but I didn't think it was in either one of our natures. Turning towards the horde, I readied myself for the end as well. I had lead a pretty good life. I had helped a lot of people. When my end finally came, it was from helping someone. Not bad for a person's karma, not bad at all. Speaking of karma...

A commotion sounded from the left side of the arena. A large set of steel doors slammed open with a sound reminiscent of a bomb going off. A man dressed in a rather nice white business suit walked onto the arena floor. He carried a long slender object over his head and the throng of demons fell away from him as if he was on fire. Without missing a step, he walked right up to Michelle and I.

"Hello Tiger," said Mediator, "this is becoming quite the habit."

"I'm not complaining," I shot back with a weak grin.

"Well, don't get any foolish notions about me being one of the good guys," he retorted, "what I do, I do for myself."

"As long as what you do for yourself gets me out of tight jams, I don't care," I said, "what's with the stick?"

"This?" he asked as he regarded the worn wood in his hand, "It's a little gift from the Roman empire."

He tossed the stick to me and I caught it in one hand. The wood felt smooth and worn. One end was flat while the other was broken to a jagged edge. The second that the stick rested in my palm, I began to feel odd sensations. Strange desires and unnamed cravings assaulted my emotions. The force of the tide of feelings washed over me, nearly driving me to the ground. Gritting my teeth, I stood upright and faced Mediator.

"What is this?" I asked again.

"You will need it," answered Mediator, "use it carefully and wisely, it exacts a terrible price for all its power."

Suddenly, Mediator disappeared. I was used to his antics but the assembled mass of demons and villains gasped at his trick. Looking over the crowd, I saw the demons shying away from me as the Succubae looked at them in disbelief. One of the women shook her head at the demons backing away from me and took it upon herself to charge at me. I sidestepped when she got near and clotheslined her. The momentum she carried flipped her completed over and she hit the ground facedown and motionless. Suddenly the throng of villains surrounding us found a pressing need to run some errands. No errand

139

in particular, just any that got them away from me.

Holding my hand out to Michelle, she grabbed it. I pulled and she was on her feet next to me. I wrapped my arm around her waist and slowly walked her out of the quickly emptying arena. As we neared one of the side doors, I heard an explosion in the distance to the south. Looking up at the amber roof, I could see faint rays of daylight brightening the sky. Then the single boom became one of many as a series of explosions rattled the building. Blizzard came earlier than he said he would.

Hurrying, I half walked and half carried Michelle from the arena. I had to slip her out the back way. She would never get out of here in the outfit she was wearing. A few times she looked up at me with weary and pained eyes as we hurried through the building. As we were nearing the back wall of the Citadel, we turned a corner into a nasty surprise.

"Give it to me," snarled Angel as she pointed at the piece of wood I carried, "give it to me and you can walk away with your woman. Refuse me at your own peril."

"Why do you want it Angel?" I asked as I slid nearer to her, "What is so important about this stick?"

"You fool. It is a weapon of power. One of only a handful still existing on this planet that can kill a divine being," she said as she eyed the stick, "the only weapon of power to be seen and used in the modern age."

"Well, if you want it so bad..." I said, holding the stick outward.

She rushed forward with her arms outstretched. As she neared me, I pulled back the stick and drove it forward with all my strength. Her headlong flight towards the prize rammed the stick deep into her side. Blood flowed from her mouth as I locked eyes with her. The light from her eyes slowly began to fail as I spoke.

"You made it personal."

Her eyes closed and she slid off the stick as she fell. Particles of light began to spiral around her and she became more transparent with each passing second. In under a minute, a tower of light stood where Angel's body had lain when it breathed it's last. A brilliant flash signaled the end of the column of light and when my eyes returned to normal, I grabbed up Michelle and continued on my way.

Carrying Michelle was easy physically but hard on my emotions. I wanted to lay her down on the cool grass and let her rest but I knew I couldn't. She needed sleep and solitude. She was all torn up inside and the one thing I had learned about women was that no man could ease that pain. It was something the woman had to do own her own. Guys were just too dumb to understand.

As we neared the exit to the park, I saw a pair of figures regarding us in the distance. A familiar blue and white suit with snowflakes next to an armored man holding a fancy gun told who the figures were. The one with the gun started towards us but the other man held him back. Looking at me and then looking at the woman I carried then back at the stick in my hand, the figure was rigid in it's introspection. Then the man in the distance looked at me and nodded his head before walking away, his companion joining him after a second. Good. One less thing to worry about this morning.

Jogging, I ate up the distance to my neighborhood before the sunlight could reach over the tops of the buildings. Early morning in my neighborhood was an almost pleasant experience. The day was still cool enough that the stench of rotten garbage hadn't filled the streets yet. The beggars and whores and hustlers were still catching forty winks or on their way to catch 'em. The only people moving about were those people who worked the early morning shift or those coming home from the late one.

Michelle did not stir as I entered my apartment building. The front desk was unmanned and empty as I passed it on my way to the stairwell. Walking up to my floor took only a minute and I passed through the doorway I had demolished earlier. Stepping into my own apartment, I carried Michelle in and laid her down on my bed. As much as I would have enjoyed unpeeling her outfit and putting her in pajamas, I just wasn't in the mood for it right now. Covering her slumbering form with a thin blanket, I quietly walked over to my table and sat down. I placed the stick in front of me and regarded it with sleepy, hooded eyes.

It exacts a terrible price for all it's power. That's what Mediator said.

141

What sort of price? I wondered. What sort of power? It sure seemed to scare the demons and it turned Angel into a laser light show. But what was it? And who was Mediator?

If I had known then what I know now, I wouldn't have asked. And if you knew, you wouldn't have blamed me.

Ragnarok and Roll

"Conflicts and feuds will break out, even between families,
and all morality will disappear. This is the beginning of the end."
—Micha F. Lindemans

The sun rose over the concrete jungle. But this sunrise was different from other sunrises. The sun wasn't usually a ball of glowing blackness. Granted, these days it did tend more towards a sickly grey-yellow. But a blacklight sunrise was taking it a bit too far. The color was almost purplish and black and red mixed by an insane Bosch. It even had a texture, like melting ice cream or dripping blood. The strange light that slithered in my window was enough to awake me but no help at all with chasing away sleep's capering fears. Was anything, really?

A small puddle of drool was the only sign that I had fallen asleep at my table. I glanced over at saw that Michelle still slept in my bed. Her warm curves rhythmically moving with her every slumbering breath. A clean white sheet covered her. Well...what passed for clean and white in my book, anyway.

I started to push away from the table and stand when my hand brushed something. The oddest feelings overtook me as my fingers closed over the stick. Lifting it up, I couldn't help myself as I regarded it with a fierce craving to use it again. Surely, I could find someone worthy of death at its tip. Whoa...That isn't me...and don't call me Shirley.

PHIL MORGAN II

Dropping the stick back on the table, I sat back down in my chair and regarded it warily. Whatever it was, it was something beyond anything I had ever handled. I wasn't so sure that I wanted to touch it again. It had grabbed control of me and pulled my puppet strings for a few seconds. And it pulled real hard. Rubbing my hands over my eyes, I leaned way back in the chair. Something fell across my knees as I was stretching.

Somehow, the stick had rolled off the table and now lay in my lap. I pulled my hands away from my eyes and stared down at it. Taking a deep breath and gritting my teeth, I grabbed the stick firmly in my right hand. The same tugging and desires and cravings washed over me like a wave as I lifted the stick and placed it back on the table. Dropping it disdainfully, I turned and walked over to the fridge. Grabbing a small container of orange juice, I drank deeply. I was trying to slake the thirst I felt, trying to hold back the craving. Slowly, the sweet, pulpy liquid cut through the film in my mouth. After a moment, I was savoring the taste of the juice and not obsessing over the stick. After a moment, I was almost myself again.

I knew what I was going to do with the stick for now. I went over to my closet and jerked the door open. Rummaging around on the shelf I finally found what I was after. I pulled out a long black leather case. Pulling open the zipper, I removed a long pool stick. Once upon a time, I fancied that I could play pool. Then I realized that I could play, just real badly. Either way, the case was perfect for the damn stick.

Crossing back over to the table, I steeled myself again and grabbed the stick. Ramming it in the case, I quickly closed the zipper. Leaning it against the table, I began to try to get ready. I located my suit, pulled it on, and grabbed up the leather case. Looking back at Michelle, I almost walked out. Instead, I went over to her, and pushed the hair out of her face. The blacklight sunshine cast an odd glamour to her face as I bent down and kissed her forehead gently. Her eyes fluttered open and she sleepily looked up at me.

"Baby?" she said softly, "Is everything ok?"

"Yeah, darling. Go back to sleep," I whispered to her.

"I love you," she said softly as she slipped back into dreamland.

"I love you too," I said as I walked out what used to be my door.

I stalked down the hallway and through the broken stairwell door. In a hurry, I jogged down the stairs and out of the building in record time. My new powers had increased my speed incredibly, almost exponentially. My normal movements now propelled me much greater distances than before. Last night, I had been operating on instinct. Now, I found myself bounding with every small step and lunging with every regular one. I eyed the doorknob I had just grabbed and saw faint indentations where my fingertips had bent the metal like warm chocolate. To tell the truth, I wasn't so sure I would ever be the same again. And I don't just mean the new superpowers.

I looked around the street I stood on, the same street I stood on everyday. Today was no different that any other day, at least it seemed that way at first. Upon further scrutiny, I saw the silent tremble in the trudging of the indigent, the sparkle of fear in the casual pedestrian. I saw the throbbing pulse in the throats of the hookers and the jittery hands of the loitering junkies. They knew. They knew that the end was near.

Almost prophetically, an old man lay unconscious next to a hand lettered sign that warned us of our impeding doom. The sign glared reproachfully at me, it's crooked lettering jangling my nerves. The end is nigh, it said. When the hell is nigh, anyway?

Regardless, of the street prophet's warning, I began to travel towards City Hall. I had woken in plenty of time, even though I only had a few scant moments of slumber. I felt as though I was moving through thick molasses or simply going through the motions. My fatigue made the leather case I carried feel as if it were made of solid lead. Maybe something other than simple fatigue played a part as well but at the moment I was more than ready to attribute the sluggish feeling in my limbs to a long night and not some supernatural means. Either way, I was damn tired and it showed.

As I moved down the block, I felt a chill wind pass through an otherwise warm morning. A chill wind that sapped my remaining strength and weaken my will caressed my flesh, killing the glow of autumn. Small flurries began to fall. The people I could see reacted with mixed expressions, ranging from sheer amazement to resigned weariness. I suppose the regular inhabitants of the city were more than used to odd occurrences. I know I was.

Picking up my pace, I passed the invisible line that marked the boundary of Lowtown. After leaving my concrete jungle, I entered a war zone. Whereas my neighborhood had escaped major destruction, the rest of the city had not been so lucky. Even inconsequential areas had been hit and they had been hit real hard. No window had been left untouched and no store unlooted. Unbelievable amounts of trash littered the sidewalk, stopping all foot traffic in some places. Several buildings in sight had been damaged in such a way that bricks had been scattered all the way across the street. Gaping holes showed how powered thugs circumvented security systems when they did not fear a response from the city's defenders. Light poles lay twisted and broken, their globes shattered beyond repair. A fire hydrant had been shattered and water flooded the street. Dodging puddles of water, I quickly passed through the neighborhood and into the next one.

The next was as bad as the first and I tried my damnedest to block out the destruction. Eventually, I reached my destination. Rounding the corner, I got my first look at what remained of City Hall. The whole time that I had spent traveling had been punctuated by an increasing downpour of fluffy snowflakes. The ground had been covered in a pristine, white blanket that hid the more gruesome aspects remaining from the day before. Wind whipped small cyclones of loose powder than danced and pranced amongst discomforting, body-like shapes. Black light made the smooth drifts glow with unearthly colors. Broken and shattered statues seemed to huddle against the sudden cold snap. I should have listened to my grandfather and become a plumber.

Unfortunately it was too late for that now and I trudged through the snow drifts towards the entrance to the building. A few half frozen and skittish heroes eyed me for a second before they recognized my costume. After they knew who I was, most didn't even try to meet my gaze. In fact, after they had stared at me for a second, they seemed to return to their misery with a vengeance. My eyes narrowed as I approached the door. Something was off, something was really wrong. Granted, a blizzard in August was not exactly a normal occurrence and a prison break was not exactly grounds for a Superhero's Ball but a little morale was still expected. At the moment, the spirit of the city's defenders was nearly broken and I wasn't so sure that I was the one to fix it. Actually, I was sure that I wasn't. Shows what I knew.

I yanked the door open and walked right into Shimmer. Again. He was the one who jumped backwards this time though. Eyeing the leather case in my hand, he backed into the wall beside me and disappeared. Whatever this thing was, it certainly had an affect on people. First the demons, then Angel, then me, and now Shimmer. Pulling my arm through the case's leather strap, I pushed it over my shoulder. My hands free, I headed towards the conference room. I had heard numerous voices in there arguing.

Pushing the door open, I saw a room full of heroes. I knew a few of them but most were unfamiliar. Jinx was there, disdainfully ignoring the other heroes. Junkyard was trying to speak at the front of the room. Gun Control and Stiletto were sitting in the back. American Eagle sat with a young girl that I didn't know. A few other heroes nodded to me or caught my eye as I pushed towards the podium where Junkyard was standing. He handed me a thick sheaf of papers as I drew near. The arguments in the room went quiet as I flipped through the information. Seems something had attacked the makeshift prison set up by the National Guard. When word had reached Centennial Park, Blizzard had taken his team on a rescue mission. Not long after, the sudden snowstorm had hit and contact with the prison camp had been lost.

"Man, I'm glad you're here," whispered Junkyard, "way too many chiefs and not enough braves in this group."

"Sounds like typical hero behavior," I replied out of the corner of my mouth, "take a seat, let's get started."

Junkyard turned and grabbed a chair with the other heroes. Fixing them with a stern glare, I singled out a few of them for special assignments. The slightly fidgety crowd grew still as I began to address them.

"The situation is grim. The prison camp was attacked and Blizzard's team went to try to help. We have lost contact with them both since this weird weather started," I explained, "I need a volunteer to fly over and get us some information."

Surprisingly, the young girl next to American Eagle stood and raised her hand. She wore a costume very similar to Eagles, old fashioned and patriotic. Eagle tried to grab her arm but she dodged him and stepped into the aisle. He started to stand as she strode towards me.

"I'll go," said the young girl, "I'm a flyer."

"No…" began Eagle.

"What is your name, young lady," I interrupted with a stern voice.

"Sparrow," she answered with a quaver in her voice, "I'm Eagle's twin sister."

"Okay, Sparrow. Go give the prison camp a flyover. Don't engage, we need information more than we need you to be a hero," I ordered.

"No, she's too young…" began Eagle again.

"Sit down," I said, my voice assuring that I would brook no arguments, "she is the same age as you are and you're not too young."

American Eagle looked as if he wanted to keep arguing but he sat down as I stared at him. His sister turned on her heels and nodded to me as she walked out the door. I understood Eagle's concern but right now, the city needed all the help it could get. Even if that help was a teenaged girl who looked just short of ridiculous in her costume. Besides, she wouldn't be any safer at home.

"Eagle, I want you and Gun Control to organize the defenses of City Hall. As of right now, City Hall is our base of operations. We need it to be as secure as possible. I do not want a repeat attack here," I ordered, "Stiletto, I need you to gather up a street sweeping team and clean up the surrounding neighborhood. I don't want anything sneaking up on us and I want any refugees to have a clean route. Jinx, you and Junkyard assemble two rapid response teams from the remaining heroes. When Sparrow returns with information, we need to be able to act upon it."

Fixing the heroes in the room with my most serious gaze, I tried to show the importance of my commands with my eyes, "I need you all to stay alert and ready. Times look real grim right now but we can make it through this. We just need to be the heroes that the people of our city expect us to be. They need us. Some of us won't make it, many of us have already fallen. Let's make that mean something. If we give up now, we are spitting on the bodies of our friends."

Looking around the room again, I stared into pale and drawn faces. I saw fear and doubt, "We are heroes. Super Heroes. That counts for something. When the times are dark and hope has fled, we are the angels that drop from the heavens to drive back the shadows. We are the ones who willingly lay down our lives to save others. We are the last hope for many. We are heroes."

I walked towards the door and opened. I spoke without turning to face the room, "Now, go out there and prove it."

The door shut behind me. As it shut, I could hear the heroes in the room I had just left moving about. Presumably to either follow my orders or stage a revolt. At this point, I didn't really care. As I began to walk away, I heard the door open behind me. I turned just as American Eagle stepped towards me.

"I'm sorry…" he began, "I'm just worried about her."

"It's okay, son. I understand how you feel but right now, I need you to concentrate on our defenses. A handful of us may need to hold here," I explained compassionately.

"It's just…my grandfather died last night," he replied, "the stress got to him, we think."

"I'm sorry," I said with genuine feeling, "I never knew him personally but his exploits were the stuff of legend."

"Yeah, they were, weren't they?" he said, his eyes sparkling with a sheen of tears.

I gave him a moment and then gently grabbed his shoulder, "You need to catch up with Gun Control. You've got a job to do."

"Thanks," he said as he wiped his eyes, "I'll get right on it."

He walked away as I watched him go. The kid was having a bad day. Hell, we were all having a bad day. Between the blacklight sunrise and the Autumn snow drifts, today certainly wasn't the Fourth of July. We were all on edge. It didn't matter that we were heroes. Some things were beyond even our abilities.

All in all, we were holding up decently. I had been pleasantly surprised that I hadn't been laughed out of the room when I was acting like I knew what I was doing. But then again, maybe the city's defenders were just glad that somebody had stepped up to the plate. Who knows?

I entered the stairwell and trudged up to the roof. I walked through the door and over to the roof's edge. Below me, I saw Gun Control working on the robotic drones. I presumed he was souping them up a bit. A few feet over, Eagle was stacking dozens sandbags into half circles. His incredible strength helping him move large numbers of the heavy bags with a single arm. In the five minutes since I had spoken to him, he had already constructed three sandbag bunkers. A pair of heroes stood guard behind each one. Over to the left side, I could see Stiletto leading a group of five other heroes across the street. The pride in their walk was visible from all the way on the roof. I suppose my little talk did help morale after all.

I didn't expect them to find anything. I had just traveled those same streets half an hour earlier and had seen no one. Still, it made them feel better to be doing something and it helped the populace to see that the heroes were still on patrol. As I was musing, I felt a cold presence come up behind me.

"What's on your mind, Shimmer?" I asked without turning.

"You," he answered in his sepulchral voice, "you have changed."

"So has this city," I replied, "I didn't have a choice in the matter. Trust me, I would rather be plain old Night Tiger. Not whatever it is that I am becoming."

"Be careful," he warned, "you carry a dangerous artifact."

"What is it? It fills me with wrath every time I touch it," I said.

"It is the Lance," he answered. "that is all the answer I am allowed to give you."

"Allowed?" I asked as I turned to him with a puzzled expression.

"Yes, Marvin. Allowed," he answered as he began to walk away, "if I could say more, I would. Just be careful with it. Only use it as a last resort."

"Otherwise, it will consume you as it has others," his last words hung in the air as he dropped through the rooftop, "many others."

Watching him disappear was no less unnerving than ever. In fact, his ominous tone and cryptic words made it even worse. What was it with these spiritual people? Why couldn't they ever just spit it out plainly? And what could keep a dead man from saying what he knew? What was that powerful?

As I asked, it dawned on me. The Lance itself was that powerful. Angel said it could kill a divine being. I supposed that meant it was one badass toy. Why the hell did Mediator give it to me in the first place?

My navel gazing was cut short when I saw a flying figure approaching from a long way off. It was Sparrow on her way back. As I began to walk back downstairs, three more figures appeared in the air behind her. They were so far behind they were tiny in comparison but they steadily followed in her wake. Somebody was chasing her. Well, they were in for a surprise.

Bounding to the edge of the roof, I called down to the heroes outside. At the sound of my voice, both Eagle and Gun Control looked up at me. Their gaze followed where I was pointing and after a moment's hesitation they began to scramble around the courtyard. By the time that the detail's in Sparrow's outdated costume were becoming visible, three sentry drones were hovering in combat mode and the heroes on guard duty below were ready for battle.

Sparrow came swooping down into the courtyard, fatigue evident on her face and in her wavering flight. Gaining on her, the three figures were clearly visible as they dove towards City Hall. Large, leathery wings beat the air as the demonic creatures screamed in rage at the assembled defenses. At a distance they were small specks of shadow, up close they were large, nasty monsters. Red flesh strained over steel hard muscles and black talons flexed in rage and hunger.

A sudden clatter sounded as Gun Control let loose a barrage of rounds from his complex weapon. The distinctive whine of the sentry drone's weapons sounded in concert with his attack. Eagle ripped up large chunks of pavement and hurled them at the demons. The other heroes unleashed with their powers and within seconds all the demons had been driven from the sky.

Leaping from the roof, I somersaulted mid-flight. I landed lightly and sprinted towards one of the grounded monsters. Its wing had been damaged by one of Eagle's boulders and hung limply from its shoulder. It snarled at me in anger as I hurtled towards it. When I got within range, it lashed out with its claws. I grabbed its hands and began to slowly bend the beast backwards. Sheer strength forced the demon to its

151

knees. It looked at me with puzzled fear in its alien face as I rammed my hands forward. Twin cracks sounded as the creatures arms broke under the strain and a ululating cry escaped its lipless mouth. The whimpering creature collapsed in agony as I turned to see that the other demons had been dispatched.

American Eagle approached the demon I had defeated and grabbed it up by its damaged wing. A sickening hiss came from the monster when it was yanked up and thrown over Eagle's shoulder. Eagle looked at me with a question in his eyes and I gestured towards City Hall.

"Put it in an empty holding tank. Send someone to banish it as soon as possible," I ordered, "then see if you sister is okay and bring her to the conference room."

"Yes, sir," was his reply as he marched into the building carrying his prisoner.

I watched him as he walked away. In my head, I could feel some presence battering away at me. You could banish it, the presence said. You have the means. You have the right. Take up the Lance and use it as it was meant to be used, it advised.

My hand was slowly creeping towards the leather case on my back when I noticed it. Forcing myself to take control of my own body, I stopped myself from grabbing the Lance. Shimmer had not been kidding. This thing was trouble, whatever it was. Its hunger had grabbed me and nearly made me its slave. Only sheer force of will had stopped me from slipping over the edge. I would have to be extra careful with the Lance. Or it would own me.

While I had a strong sense of vengeance, I was also adamantly against wholesale slaughter. I could already feel the Lance affecting me however, and my bloodlust for retribution had been rising since the first moment I had grasped its smooth surface. Even now, my conscience struggled mightily with the aspects of myself that wanted absolute justice with unfettered vengeance and the ones that wanted peaceful protection of the innocent.

All these thoughts and a thousand more danced behind my eyes as I began to walk towards the building. By the time I reached the door, the ghosts of the insinuations still burned in my mind. Vague, formless, and ephemeral, the desire snuck back into the shadows of my thoughts.

Still perturbed, I eventually reached the conference room. Opening the door, I saw Eagle talking with his sister while Junkyard and Jinx sat and watched. When the door closed behind me, Junkyard looked up at me and nodded. Jinx did what she always does, she ignored me. Eagle stopped talking to his sister but sat with his hand protectively resting on her shoulder. Sparrow looked at me with hollow eyes and a strained face.

"Are you okay?" I asked her, ignoring the others in the room.

"I'll be alright. I just need to catch my breath," she said shakily.

"Take your time, little lady," I offered, "I know it was bad."

"Bad doesn't even come close…" she said, letting her sentence trail off.

"It's okay, you're safe now," said Eagle with concern in his voice.

"No!" snapped Sparrow as she brushed his hand from her shoulder, "You didn't see what I saw. You don't know what I know. It is NOT going to be okay."

Eagle leaned back in shock at his sister's outburst. Sparrow stared at him with a powerful look of defiance in her eyes. She has spirit, I thought, that's for sure. Slowly tearing her eyes from her brother, she looked at me and began to speak in a low voice.

"I got near the prison camp and could see smoke from a lot of fires. I circled above and saw dead bodies and fires everywhere. On my second pass, I saw some movement and landed to check it out," she said, "it was one of the soldiers. He was dying from a belly wound. I saw him as he was trying to crawl under a burned out jeep."

"Go on," I said when she paused in her recollection.

"He told what happened 'fore he died. He said that the camp had been holding most of the maximum security prisoners from the Tower. He said that many of them had still been in their cells when the Guard checked out what left of the prison," she explained, "he said that a monster showed up this morning, a giant demon, standing over 40 feet tall. With the monster came hordes of smaller demons and monsters. The soldier said they ripped through the camp with ease, freeing the prisoners."

"Which ones," I asked.

"A lot of bad guys," she said as she handed my a torn and bloody piece of paper, "he gave me this before he died."

As I looked over the paper, my eyes widened in shock. Listed were the baddest, evilest, craziest villains in the history of the city. Graveyard, Replicant, the Piper, Bloodmoon, they were all a match for the city's heroes all by themselves. All of them on the loose at the same time was a nightmare made real.

"My god..." I stammered.

"That bad?" asked Junkyard as he reached for the paper in my numb fingers.

"See for yourself," I answered as I let him take the list, "Sparrow, any information about Blizzard and his team?"

"The soldier said that they showed up as the Demon was attacking," she said with her eyes downcast, "he said the demon killed Blizzard and a massive snowstorm appeared. The others were ripped apart, I saw some of the bodies."

"When the soldier died, I began to snoop around. I guess I made too much noise and a couple of demons appeared from under the snow," she continued, "I flew as fast as I could but they chased me until I got here."

"You did good," I said, "rest for a bit and then find your brother. He will find a place for you here. A safe place."

"Eagle, you need to get back to the defenses," I ordered as I began to stand.

Jinx and Junkyard were pouring over the list that Sparrow brought back. I gave them a moment to let it set in as Eagle and Sparrow left the room. When I cleared my throat, Junkyard looked up at me with genuine fear in his eyes. Jinx just looked bored.

"What are we supposed to do?" demanded Junkyard, "I fought against Replicant years ago. Thirty heroes went after him. He nearly killed us and he is the weakest one on the list."

"I know," I said, "our only option is to wait for one of them to pop up and hit him or her real hard. Make sure your teams are ready to go at a moment's notice and make damn sure that they are well versed with how to handle each of the possible super villains."

They both nodded to me and got up to leave. As the door shut behind them, I sat down in the leather chair at the front of the room. I was tired. My eyes felt like they had been rolled in a sandbox and stuck back in the sockets. A funny taste filled the back of my mouth, it was odd, almost coppery. My fingers twitched nervously. The butterflies in my stomach seemed to be playing a game of tackle football and cold sweat rolled down the small of my back. What was I going to do? Then it hit me...

Fimbulwinter Wonderland

"Is it cold in here?"
—anonymous

Shady Pines Cemetery was located near Centennial Park. Covering over twenty acres, it was one of the larger graveyards in the city. Tasteful, wrought iron gates shut out the hustle of the outside world. Then a sullen squeak cried sadly as a figure pushed the gates open. Even though the weird afternoon sunlight cast a strange glow on the figure, its features remained hidden in the shadows that seemed to cling to it. Tattered strips of orange cloth hung from its emaciated form. Yellowed claws flexed and danced over the marble headstones as the figure walked slowly through the rows. A strange hush fell over the already quiet cemetery. Light seemed to retreat and an odd wind suddenly began to stir the red and gold leaves on the ground. A low moan sounded as a skeletal hand burst through the ground of a nearby grave. Within a minute, a chorus of moaning bodies began to rise from the once silent ground. The shadowy figure continued its stroll through the bone yard, bodies reanimating behind its every step.

The streets of Crystal Lake were quiet and empty after the troubles of the night before. Only a few children were outside to witness her arrival. A riot of colors decorated her garish costume. She raised the strange flute she carried to her lips. Taking a deep breath, hypnotic polytonal music began to flow from her instrument. The children had begun to edge away when she first appeared at the end of the street. As she started playing, they took on a look of pure blankness. Grabbing sticks, and baseball bats, the children began to follow woodenly in her wake as other children swarmed out of nearby buildings. Each of them carried some sort of weapon, some dripping blood.

A non-descript man walked into Nails and Stuff hardware store. He walked into the center aisle and looked at the rows of crowbars and pry bars. He reached for one and there was a quick, popping noise. Another non-descript man was suddenly standing next to the first holding a crowbar, looking exactly like the first. The first man then reached for another of the tools and the noise sounded again. Now, three men stood there. The first looked at the other two, grinned, and reached for another crowbar.

The shadowed alleyway was perfect cover for him. He hated the light of day. Today was no different even if the light was different. He still preferred the loving glow of the full moon. It filled him with silver shine and made him feel like he was the god of the wolves. And maybe he was. Leaping powerfully from the shadow, his claws left white scars in the concrete where he landed. Reaching out, he grabbed a light post and ripped it from the sidewalk. Holding the still sparking pole over his head, he leaned his head back and howled. Windows shattered on the quiet street and a few seconds later answering howls sounded in the distance. Snuffling sounds preceded the arrival of the first of the pack. His ears perked up as the smaller gray wolf appeared at the corner. Its head was bowed low as it slunk towards him. When it lay sniveling before him, the others began to appear. The pack was here.

Agzamoth was pleased. His demons were bringing him plenty of meat, squirming and screaming. Their souls were bloating his body and increasing his power. Looking over the ruined Citadel, he was even more pleased. Whoever had attacked here had saved him the trouble. These foolish humans believed they would be placed high in his kingdom and never had the slightest idea that he was more of a pawn than a king. And as such being the case, the ones who summoned him here would have made tasty snacks if someone else had not beaten him to it. He wasn't angry though. There were plenty of snacks in this world.

A small house sat on a side street. There was nothing remarkable about the house from the outside. On the inside, the house stood mainly empty. Only two rooms had anything to speak of in them. The kitchen contained several weeks worth of food and drink. The bedroom had a single bed with a man sleeping in it. All around the bed were motion detectors. A red light began to blink on one, then another, then all of the detectors. The man in the bed slowly sat upright and began to rub his eyes. He looked at the clock next to his bed and slowly frowned. Someone had woken him up early and someone would pay for it.

I had just finished with my plan when the red light over the comm unit went off. The red light that every hero who worked in City Hall knew about and hoped to never see light up. So far, in my years of crime fighting it had only lit up once. It had taken every hero in the city nearly a solid day to handle it then, now there was nothing we could do. I would send for my unofficial lieutenants and tell them. The Insomniac was awake and the only thing to do was get out of his way.

Hours passed quietly. Word had been passed around and everyone knew to not fight the Insomniac. Hopefully, he would just stay at home for a while and eat Fruit Loops. He probably wouldn't. Stiletto returned to City hall and informed me that her team had cleaned up the surrounding streets with ease. I sent her back out and told her to have her team patrol for refugees. They would be coming. I told them all to be ready. I said that when it happens, it will happen quickly. I was right.

The sun was about to set when the first people began to trickle in through the still falling snow. Appearing in the dusk, they came from the direction of Crystal Lake. They told of hearing strange music right before their children went crazy and ran away. Junkyard's team immediately set off after the Piper to take her down.

Before the dust had settled from their leaving, more panicked people began showing up from the direction of Gateway Mall. A huge group of men were marching towards City Hall after supposedly ransacking the stores. Supposedly all the men wore the same outfit, an orange jumpsuit. Jinx led her team after Replicant with vengeance in her eyes. Ransacking the mall was a bad idea with Jinx around.

I watched them go from the roof of City Hall. Only the sentries below and Stiletto's team were left to answer the call when it came. And it would come, it was only a matter of time. I had taken steps to help but there was no way of knowing if my plan would work. I could only watch.

The mob of children moved through the street. The strange music wafted around them and they mechanically capered and danced to its creepy melody. The children's vacant eyes and slack faces were in direct contrast with the surreal image of play they tried to mimic. The weapons in their hands ranged from sports equipment to eating utensils. Their most deadly weapon was their unquestioned innocence. The Piper played from the middle of the children, her costume sickening to watch with its motley colors.

Junkyard watched the mob from the roof of a small bookstore. He had positioned Mr. Excellent at the end of the street. He was the bait, his short term strength should be able to withstand the attacks of the children. Excellent would simply stand there and let the children attack him without hurting them. Lady Artemis was on an adjacent roof waiting for her and Myrmidon's part. When Excellent got Piper's attention, Myrmidon was going to assault the villain's mind while Artemis took out her instrument. Junkyard caught Excellent's eye and nodded.

Mr. Excellent stepped into the center of the street. He planted his feet loudly on the pavement and struck a pose of heroic proportions. The Piper's song stumbled for a split second when she noticed the hero blocking the street. Then the notes changed and became ominous. The laughter of the children grew insidious and vile, their little faces twisted into masks of hate. Rushing forward on their little feet, the children swarmed around Excellent who stood still in their midst. As soon as the children around Piper thinned, an arrow flew through the air. Piper froze in her tracks as the arrow knocked the instrument to the pavement where it shattered. Piper's eyes dilated and her knees collapsed under her. She fell limply to the street as the children began to waken from their stupor and cry in confusion.

Interface and Triage had been kept in reserve due to their relative lack of power. Instead, they were a godsend when it came to calming the scared children. Triage went among them fixing minor scrapes and bruises while Interface pulled out a miniature dvd projector and began showing the Lion King on the side of a building. Soon, the children had calmed and were watching the movie almost quietly. Child Services soon arrived to help get the children home. While they worked, Junkyard called in to report and paled when he heard the news.

"Let's go," he said to the group, "there's trouble."

Jinx's team reached the Mall just as a large mob of men were marching through the parking lot. Swooping down on the mob, the team hit the ground running. Jinx stood at the back, fire in her eyes. Sunbeam cast widespread blasts of bright sunlight as the Bubbler tried to enclose the men in clear bubbles. Roughneck leapt along the edge of the mob, hacking and slashing with each bound. Storm Front summoned whipping winds and driving rain to push the mob back. While the other heroes attacked the mob of duplicates, Vertigo was frantically searching for the mind of the true Replicant. Each duplicate that fell would disappear with a small popping noise.

Even with the might of the heroes slamming into the mass of figures, the mob was barely slowed by the assault. Roughneck got clipped by a baseball bat and stumbled. Blinded or not, enough of the duplicates could see to swarm at Sunbeam. The Bubbler barely held back the wave of men with his force field. Storm Front was able to keep back the duplicates that surrounded her but she would tire quickly. Jinx stood near Vertigo as sweat began to pop out on her forehead from the strain of her search. Suddenly, Vertigo cried out and fell to the pavement of the parking lot.

"He is the one without a weapon," she said as she grabbed at Jinx's arm. Blood began to slowly trickle out of her nose and she passed out as Jinx searched the crowd. There, she thought.

Walking straight towards the one man who was unarmed, Jinx's power began to affect the replicants. All around her men began to trip on their own feet and injure themselves with their own weapons. As she drew near the man in her sights, he turned to look at her. Immediately, the duplicates formed a circle around the two.

"Just the little lady I wanted to see," said Replicant, "I couldn't stop thinking about you since I saw you on TV yesterday."

"You don't scare me," she shot back.

"Oh, I'm sure I don't. Now," he replied, "but you don't know me yet. Wait until you and I have hung out for a bit."

"We aren't going to have the chance to hang out..." Jinx began.

"Don't be so sure, little one. I came here to draw you to me. You see..." he said with a mad gleam in his eyes, "I am not like those other supervillains. I'm not in this for money or to rule the world. I enjoy doing things to pretty young women. Bad things."

Jinx started to back away as Replicant circled towards her. His eyes tracked her as did the eyes of his duplicates. Slowly they began to circle around her in a dizzying pattern. Past the mob surrounding the two of them, she could see her team struggling with the other duplicates. She could smell him as began to speak again, his sick gaze making her flesh crawl.

"Me and my boys have such plans for you, pretty one. We want to hear your screams and feel your pain," he laughed, "we bet you look beautiful when you cry."

Jinx's lip curled in an expression that can only be described as pure hate. A weird glow appeared around her eyes as her fingers began to twitch. Replicant suddenly lost his air of confidence as the pavement under his feet began to ripple and shake.

"You wanted me? Well, now you have me!" said Jinx as she thrust her hands to the sky.

The snowfall that began that morning had not stopped all day. Until now. The second that Jinx raised her hands to the sky, the snowstorm stopped as if someone had hit a switch. The duplicates began to shy away from the pretty girl as a sharp smell of ozone began to fill the area. Replicant stared wide eyed at Jinx as she rotated to face him.

"You think you were tricking me into coming here?" she snarled, "I volunteered asshole."

Lightning struck with such ferocity that dozens of duplicates were incinerated in the first instance. Chunks of pavement rose up as the ground shook in fury. Wicked winds swirled around men, lifting them up and smashing them down. Jinx stood in the middle of the elemental fury as if she were the thunder goddess herself. Powerful forces drove nearly everyone to the ground. Within mere moments, silence reigned as Jinx and Replicant stood alone in the parking lot. Replicant looked at Jinx long and hard. And then he passed out.

The other heroes looked at Jinx with shock in their faces. A little fear was also evident in their eyes. She looked around at the heroes with her and a small smile played on her lips.

"They don't call me Jinx for nothing," she said.

While Jinx and Junkyard were leading their teams to battle, the first refugees began to bring tales of an army of monsters led by a giant demon. I sent for Stiletto and she hurried her team back to City Hall. When she got there, we went on a tour of the defenses set up by Gun Control and Eagle. They had arranged sandbag bunkers in semi circles all around the building. Heroes had been stationed in each of the bunkers, their eyes constantly scanning the snowy afternoon. Several groups of battle drones flew overhead while a few teams of robotic soldiers marched around. Three weapon pods were placed on the roof of the Hall, each bristling with rocket launchers and energy cannons. The falling snow would lessen the effectiveness of the mechanized defenses but hopefully not too much.

By the time Stiletto and I had completed our tour, the number of refugees arriving was staggering. All brought crazy sounding stories of Hell on earth and armies of monsters. Sadly, they weren't crazy. It was hell on earth, the end of the world, judgment day. Oh well, let's Ragnarok and Roll!

The first groups of demons to come into view paused as they saw us. After a moment, they charged across the empty street and towards the building. A flight of battle drones picked them up immediately and swooped down on them. Energy cannons raked the handful of demons, several falling to the first barrage. The second pass took out the rest of the demons except for the largest. It weathered several shots from the drones and kept coming. The drones turned in a tight arc and swooped back towards the monster. As they neared, a crafty light entered the demon's eyes and it spun towards the drones. Leaping into the sky, the demon slammed into one of the drones and brought it to the ground. Rolling with the impact, the demon staggered upright and threw the damaged machine at another. The two drones impacted in midair and a powerful explosion rocked the demon to it's knees. Before it could rise, the remaining three drones burned it to a crisp with their weapons. The assembled heroes and civilians let forth a ragged cheer when the last demon fell. I turned to Stiletto with a look of genuine fear in my eyes.

"What?" she whispered as the heroes cheered.

"We won't make it through this at this rate," I said as I shook my head slightly, "we can't afford to lose two drones for every five demons destroyed. There is going to be a lot more than five attacking us soon."

Stiletto's teeth clenched as she considered what I had just said. Her eyes closed and her head bowed for a second. I grew concerned for her as she just stood there motionless for a solid minute. When she looked up at me, the sheen of tears in her eyes were clear as day.

"You're right," she said hoarsely, "but we don't have any choice. There is nothing we can do, nowhere for us to run, and nobody coming to save us."

"Well, we can fight. We can fight them right here. And I wouldn't be so sure that nobody is coming," I grinned cryptically.

"What do you mean?" she asked.

"I sent out a distress call before Junkyard and Jinx left," I said, "we might have some friendly company on the way."

"Who'd you call?" she asked.

"You'll see when they get here. For now, make sure your team is in place to plug any holes in the defenses. You are the "flying" company. It's your job to be where we need you before we even know we need you there. And we WILL need you," I ordered, "got it?"

"Yessir," she said with a sarcastic grin as she walked away.

I watched her go for a moment before I turned back to scan the defenses. My eyes searched constantly for that one weak spot, that one place where the enemy could walk right through. City Hall was full of the citizens of the city. All of them were terrified and exhausted. We had to hold for them. We had too.

While I scanned for gaps, I noticed Shimmer standing on the roof near one of the weapon pods. He was staring intently at me as if he was willing me to look at him. Hell, maybe he was. When he saw me looking at him, he motioned curtly to me. Nodding once in response, I walked towards the building. The defenders watched me as I went and I tried to catch as many of their gazes as possible. I tried with each fleeting glance to convey how important this was. I tried to tell them with my eyes to stand firm. Maybe they got it and maybe they didn't. I reached the roof quickly once I got inside the building. Shimmer was standing in the same place where he had motioned. He spoke to me without turning to face me.

"Stand up here with me, my friend," he said, "heh. A ghost having a friend…I am the laughing stock of the afterlife."

"I resent that Shimmer. I'm not that bad of a friend to have," I said jokingly.

"No. No, you aren't," he said as he looked sideways at me, "in fact, you are such a good friend that I am going to try to save you."

"Save me?" I laughed, "How are you going to save me, Shimmer."

"By keeping you up here with me and not down there where the Lance would force you to use it," he said with all seriousness, "no matter how strong your willpower is, even you couldn't stop the Lance from being used in the type of battle that is coming."

"So, I should stay up here with you during the fight?" I asked.

"Yes. As bad as it gets, it will only be worse if the Lance tastes too much blood," said Shimmer in a faraway voice, "the Lance is bloodthirsty…yes…very bloodthirsty."

"Shimmer…" I began.

"Hmm?" he said, "Sorry, I drifted off there for a second. One of the drawbacks of being a ghost I suppose."

"If you say so…" I trailed off.

Shimmer and I watched the quiet streets for a few minutes before the first signs of what was to come appeared. Flocks of pigeons began to suddenly take to the sky in the east. A strange rumbling sound began to rise up from the streets and alleys. With the sound came an uncontrollable dread that settled in the pit of our stomachs. Something was coming. We could all feel it. Even from the roof, I could see white knuckles clutching sandbags and nervous twitches rippling through the defenders. Even the robots seemed nervous, stumbling here and there in their marionette's waltz. Then we could see them.

Lines of them, hordes of them, a multitude of monsters came pouring out of the gloom. All shapes, all sizes, they were all horrible to see. Capering imps marched next to slouching demons who followed huge fiends. Crowding the skies over their heads were smaller flying monsters.

The flyers came first. They swooped down at the Hall in undisciplined waves. The robotic drones and soldiers began to acquire them as targets and started firing at them. The weapon pod started tracking them but none came within their range. Under the concerted response from the drones and sentries, the flying demons either fell back or were destroyed in midair. The solid wall of monsters gave a loud and horrible cry at the flyers being forced to retreat and started marching forward. Heroes with long range capabilities and the mechanized weapons began unleashing on the advancing monsters but for each that fell another three took its place. Quickly the monsters ate up the distance between the sandbags and the street. Snarling monsters crashed into the barriers and the battle was joined.

I saw Gun Control standing behind one of the bunkers, his weapon firing so quickly that heat shimmer was visible around its barrel. American Eagle stood in the vanguard of defenders crushing any demon who came near. His sister flew overhead with a flight of battle drones, the two energy pistols in her hands firing like she was in a Chow Yun Fat movie. I saw a slender young girl called Catscratch slashing and leaping among the imps. Beside her was Freezeflame alternately burning and freezing the monsters. All around, heroes of every stripe were kicking some serious demonic ass. All that changed quickly, though.

Someone fell, whoever it was doesn't matter. A lot of heroes fell that day. Stiletto's team rushed in to fill the gap. While they were rushing to help, another hero fell and the demons poured through the hole. I steeled myself to leap from the roof and push back the monsters when Shimmer's ghostly hand appeared in front of me.

"Wait," he said, "not yet."

As he said that I noticed him watching the door to City Hall. Suddenly, that door burst open and dozens of men rushed outside. Each man carried a standard issue energy cannon from the Hall's armory. Unbelievably, they lined up like British soldiers from the Revolutionary War and aimed the weapons at the onrushing monsters. One man yelled "Fire!" and the men all let loose on the demons. Firing rapidly, the men forced back the demons rushing through the hole and Stiletto was able to send some of her team to man the bunker. After the heroes were back in place, the men retreated back into the building. I looked at Shimmer with a question in my eyes.

"Did you think I only stood around giving cryptic statements?" he said with a transparent grin, "I gave them the cannons and told them what to do. I tried to keep it as simple as possible. When you see the whites of their eyes and all...though, I suppose I should have said red of their eyes instead..."

"If I could clap you on the back right now, I would," I said with a grin, "that was a great idea. I should've thought of it."

After the civilians had pushed back the demons and the heroes had retaken the bunker, I spent a minute looking over the battlefield. The wave of demons had fallen back and only a few would charge at the bunkers at a time. Most of the robotic defenses had fallen but had taken an amazing toll on the demons. A few heroes had fallen, either dead or unable to fight, among them were Freezeflame, Catscratch, and a hero called Bumrush. Bumrush and Freezeflame had been killed when the bunker had been overrun and Catscratch had been knocked unconscious by a pair of imps. A hero named Slither had used his elastic body to snatch her from the claws of the monsters, getting a slight concussion in the process. Hundreds of demons and imps had fallen in the first wave of the battle and still the mob attacking City Hall looked unchanged. Behind the demons and imps rushing mindlessly at the barricades stood the fiends. Bigger, stronger, and smarter, they were like the demon I had fought in the Citadel's arena last night. They were bad news. The way they stood back and watched told me that they were throwing monsters at us to see what was the best way to break our defenses. Hungry, angry demons are bad enough. When they are hungry, angry, devious, and smart, it's even worse.

One of the larger fiends gave a sudden howl and the massive throng of monsters stopped attacking the barricades. As the howl continued, the demons began to back away and slink back to the fiends. The heroes relaxed slightly as the demons and imps assembled around their larger counterparts. I didn't relax. Whatever they were up to, it wasn't going to be good. They didn't need a breather. No, they had something else up their sleeves.

The larger fiend howled again, this time was more blood curdling than the last. The hundreds possibly thousands of diminutive imps in the crowd began to scamper away. Sadly for them, they weren't fast enough. Before the last note of the howl died, the demons began to grab up the imps and savagely eat them alive. The screams of the imps were horrific to hear, even worse the attacking demons began to grow into larger, more deadly, fiends. Most of the defenders either turned away in fear or disgust at the spectacle, some were violently sick at the carnage. All were shaken. Even me.

When the cries of the imps became infrequent, I looked back at the bloodbath. The demons who had partaken in the slaughter were now full grown fiends. The original fiend began a strange hooting and the new ones looked towards us. Before we could even comprehend fully, the fiends began to slowly move towards the barricades. The mob of demons had originally been huge. In it's place stood a much smaller group of fiends. Instead of thousands, we faced nearly a hundred. We were in trouble.

Luckily, most of the heroes had gotten their wind back and were as ready as they could be. The armed civilians had slowly filed out during the carnage and now took up positions near the door. More civilians came out to join them, also armed with energy cannons. When the first fiend got into range, the civilians started firing to deadly effect. The robotic drones and sentries had been good, the humans were devastating. Standing behind a few dozen superheroes, they had enough cover to cut down nearly half of the fiends before they reached the barricade. The fiends who remained slammed into the first bunker and American Eagle leapt over it at them. Grabbing one demon's head in each hand, he lifted them both off their feet and violently crushed both skulls with a simple squeeze. He grinned as he slammed the bodies to the ground. Gun Control popped up from the bunker and began firing large white rounds at the demons. The rounds would explode upon impact and splash some liquid all around. Each monster that a single drop landed on burst into flaming ruin. Other heroes joined in and quickly the monsters were routed. They ran back the way they came and didn't stop until the still falling snow obscured their outlines.

"That went better than expected," said Shimmer as he glanced at me.

"It'll get worse before this is over with," I said, "that was just the first battle. The war hasn't even begun yet."

I stalked off the roof. I had things to do. Maybe I couldn't fight. But there were other things I could do. I could organize and plan strategy. I could carry supplies and help the wounded. I could teach those damn civilians how to hide behind the bunkers instead of standing in a row like tin soldiers. Eh, probably not. I'm not Superman, you know.

By the time I had reached the conference room, a few heroes were already inside. Sitting exhaustedly in the chairs were Gun Control, American Eagle, Sparrow, and Stiletto. Gun Control was loading his white rounds into a large clip. Sparrow was ashen and looked worn out. Eagle was absentmindedly rubbing various bumps and bruises on his body, it was easy to see that he wasn't used to being injured. Stiletto was slowly sharpening one of her gleaming daggers as she grinned at me.

"Sitting this one out, Stripes?" she said tauntingly

"As if you needed the help!" I shot back with a grin, "Look! Your shoes aren't even scuffed from all the ass kicking!"

The other heroes all laughed at our back and forth sparring and, as usual, the laughter rejuvenated them somewhat. Fixing them with a firm gaze, I nodded my pleasure. That seemed to help even more than the feeble attempt at humor.

"Listen, I can only fight as a last resort. Some mystical mumbo-jumbo," I explained lamely, "you guys have to pull this one out. I'm the last line of defense."

"Well, we did okay out there," said Gun Control.

"Yeah, this time," shot back Stiletto.

"She's right. They will be back. Plus, there were reports of a really big one with some of them," said Eagle.

I nodded at them, "It's true. His name is Agzamoth."

"So, basically all we have to worry about is one army of demons and one really big demon leading them?" asked Sparrow sarcastically, "no problem, no freaking problem at all."

"You wish. There is also the little matters of Bloodmoon and Graveyard and the Insomniac," I smiled evilly, "we haven't heard a word about them...but we will before this is all over with."

"What is going on?" demanded Stilleto, "You know Tiger. Tell us what's going on."

"Haven't you figured it out yet?" I said as I walked to the door, "Can't you see it?"

I turned back to them with my hand grabbing the door handle. I gave them a sad smile that told them volumes before I even spoke. They knew it, just like the bums in my neighborhood knew it. But they were going to make me tell them anyway.

"It's the end of the world," I said as I left the room.

Stiletto caught up with me before I could take half a dozen steps. Boy, she can hustle in those high heeled boots! She reached out to grab my shoulder and I pivoted suddenly and leaned against a nearby desk. She caught herself before she stumbled and glared at me reproachfully.

"What did you mean in there 'It's the end of the world'," she mimicked me.

"I meant what I said sweetheart," I stared at her, "I saw the writing on the wall when I woke up this morning."

"That doesn't answer my question. Why is it the end of the world?" she demanded.

"Who knows? What I do know is that in the last week I have seen anarchy like never before. Armies of goons fighting in the streets, demons and immortals vying for power, mystical objects and prophecies at every turn," I said as I picked up a small statue from the desk, "I mean, this time last week, I was wearing Kevlar armor and jump kicking thugs. This week..."

I looked at the statue in my hand. It was made of bronze and looked vaguely familiar. I could feel a plague on the other side and I flipped the statue over in my hands. The plaque read "Hero of the Year: Straight Arrow". I smiled my sad smile. Poor Straight Arrow, I could still remember seeing him throw his bow at the thugs who murdered him.

"This week," I repeated as I crushed the bronze statue like crumpling up a piece of paper, "I don't know what I am. Something both more than and less than I once was."

I tossed the ball of bronze to Stiletto and turned to leave. Her words caught me. "Great. The world is about to end, demons are marching in the streets, and you think you are a philosopher."

"Hell, girl, scratch any superhero who has worn the cape long enough and you will find a philosopher. A cheesy philosopher...but a philosopher!" I grinned back at her.

She smiled at my back. I could feel it's warmth. She would be okay out there. Unlike some of the other heroes, I felt she would make it. After all, valkyries tend to be busy during the apocalyptic battles. Someone had to carry all those warriors to Valhalla. Yeah, I've read a book before. Try not to faint.

I crossed the room to where the civilians who had joined in the battle sat nervously. Walking over to them, I simply stood before them and let them all see me. Quickly, all of them were looking at me expectantly and a few even seemed to perk up like they were at attention. I leaned on the desk behind me and in doing so brushed a paper onto the floor. I leaned down and grabbed the paper and set it back on the desk. My desk. Oh, what the hell? One of these days, I'm going to have to really learn the layout of this building. It might even help me stop looking like an idiot every time I turn around. But probably not.

I grabbed my chair and swung it around. I straddled it like a teenager channeling James Dean in Rebel with a Cause. I grinned at the men in front of me and they began to relax. I crossed my arms on the back of the chair before I began to address them.

"Well, it's about Goddamn time!" I said energetically, "I have only been waiting for you guys to step up to the plate for ten years as a hero in this city. And now I see that you were just waiting until we really needed you!"

They all laughed and a few began to jostle their neighbors. I gave them a few moments of feeling good about themselves. Hell, they earned it and a lot more. I realized right then and there that if we made it out of this I was going to lobby to have civilians given a more active role in crime fighting. They could handle it. If they could handle today like they did, they could handle anything some shoplifter threw at them.

"Now, don't go getting all full of yourselves. You won't be able to lift those cannons from all the swelling!" I grinned at them as they chuckled again. God, I love a captive audience! "Listen, you did good out there but we need you more now than ever. This isn't over with. Not by a long shot. If you can find any more who want to help, they are welcome. Arm them and send them outside."

I stood up and began to pace in front of the men. "I don't care if they are men or women, young or old, fat or thin. If they can lift one of those cannons and are willing to use it, line 'em up. A couple of you go and try to drum up some people from the refugee groups. The rest of you, follow me."

I grinned again at them as I began to walk away. "I'm going to teach you how to fight. I should be able to do a better job than the ghost. At least I'm still alive. For now."

The men followed me outside, except for a couple who went towards the refugee groups in search of more recruits. About fifty men lined up behind the sand bunkers and I began to show them how to sight their weapons. We had gone through about 10 minutes of instruction when Gun Control wandered up with thirty more men. He made them join in with the others and took over showing the men how to operate the weapons. I let him do it, I felt he would be better at it than I would. After he showed up, I walked the perimeter of the bunkers and scanned hopelessly into the increasing gloom of the evening. The snowstorm was worsening and the defenders huddled against the unnatural chill.

The quiet brought by the snowstorm was an almost palpable thing. It felt like a cold wet blanket that smothered the noise around it, almost like a true to life snow globe. Nothing else seemed to exist beyond some imaginary boundary. A strange sound to the west broke through the barrier to reach my questioning ears. I strained to make out the noise but it melded with the howl of the wind and I couldn't identify it. It was a moaning whisper chased by the screaming storm, dancing at the edges of my hearing. I didn't like it.

The moon peeked through the gathered snow clouds above me. Beams of moonlight bathed the falling flakes. Silver light cut through the sheets of snow like the rays of heaven. A deep-throated howling sounded from the south, quickly followed by an astounding chorus of howls. For a split second, the light of the moon became red, the deep red of pooling blood. Then the second passed and the moon was as it should be. Great.

A hellish glow began to appear in the dark night. The northern sky began to brighten with the same purplish-black that the sun had given all day. The color made the falling snow appear surreal and slightly maddening. With the glow came a shivering and creeping terror that seemed to grip the spine and twist it savagely. I had a pretty good idea what that was coming from and it was bad news. Really bad news.

From the east came a man. Wearing a simple bathrobe over bunny pajamas, the man walked through the drifts as if they didn't exist. His pink slippers knocked the mounds of snow and occasionally mounds of concrete aside with casual indifference. His blank and hollow eyes caught mine and he veered towards me. Silent menace preceded him and I experienced something that was rare for me. The urge to run away like a frightened schoolgirl.

"Who woke me?" demanded the man in a hollow voice.

"Not me, man," I said with only a slight tremble in my voice, "not any of us. We know better."

"Somebody did," replied the Insomniac, "I'm staying here until you find out who did."

"Umm...Just don't kill us," I said as he sat down on the stone steps in front of the building, "please."

"No promises," he answered flatly.

"Good enough," I said, "I'm glad we had this little chat."

I quickly walked away before he decided to destroy me. The Insomniac was a powerhouse. Superhuman strength way out of the league of any hero or villain in the city. Speed and reflexes that made him appear to actually teleport when he decided to move quickly. Virtually indestructible and immune to magic and poison, he was almost a god walking. The thing about the Insomniac was that he hated sleeping and hated waking up even more. When he would awaken, he would fight sleep for as long as he could. After a long while doing this, he literally began to go into suspended animation. Now, when he is woken early he tended to get a mite upset. He knew that he wasn't out long enough and would have to go back to sleep soon. And that sort of thing can really piss the guy off.

I could feel his eyes on me and hear the tendons in his neck creak slowly as he watched me go. Every step I took away from him was another step in which I was alive. That was a good enough reason to me to keep walking. I reached a spot about a dozen feet from him and raised my hands to my face.

"Hey! Did any of you do anything to wake up the Insomniac?" I yelled.

Nobody answered aloud but a few people shook their heads in fear. "Well, find out who did!" I yelled again.

I looked back at the Insomniac and said "When we know, you will."

He nodded, "Good, I might not have to kill you all then."

"I suppose I shouldn't expect anything better than that." I replied.

"No, you shouldn't," he said as he stared off to the north, "what's with the sky over there?"

"Don't ask," I said as I walked past him into the building.

I didn't feel like getting into a discussion about the end of the world with a guy who might take something the wrong way and speed up the process. The Insomniac was exactly that kind of guy. The other heroes knew not to get anywhere near him and I hoped that they stayed true to that. We needed everyone we could get and anyone who crossed the Insomniac wouldn't be useful for much more than organ donations. If even that.

I walked into the building and headed straight for the comm station. When I got there, I wasted no time in updating the automatic signal to let Jinx and Junkyard and anyone else who called what was up at City Hall. Hopefully, Jinx and Junkyard's teams had been successful in their missions. Hopefully, they were on their way back here. We needed the reinforcements.

As I finished modifying the comm message, a series of concussions sounded outside. Turning to the stairs, I rushed to the roof. Shimmer was already there when I arrived. He sure was fast when he wanted to be. I guess being able to walk through walls really cuts down on travel time.

The few drones left were firing rockets into a massive army of corpses. The undead marched towards City Hall like a barbarian horde of old. From walking skeletons to the freshly killed, they were a ghastly sight to behold. The rocket fire unleashed upon them destroyed many but the zombies shuffled on unperturbed. As they entered the range of the heroes and armed militia, the undead began to surge ahead. As they charged, every defender able to let loose with everything they had. Uncountable zombies fell and still they pushed onward. As the wave of corpses hit the first line of barricades a chilling howl cut through the falling snow.

Bounding towards the defenses came what could only be described as a giant werewolf. Running at full speed to keep up the monster, a huge pack of wolves tore through the snow. The monster, Bloodmoon, leapt upon a sandbag bunker and flattened one of the heroes trying to attack him. Turning his head upwards to face the moon he howled again.

A keening laughter filled the night air. Straight below me the Insomniac sat and roared in uncontrollable mirth as the world unraveled around him. Zombie hordes in front of him, Fenris reincarnate on his right, this sort of thing always hit his funny bone. He was virtually indestructible and he knew it. Combine that with an almost sociopath personality and it was no wonder he found this so funny. I really hated that guy.

The purple blacklight from the north grew to such intensity that night nearly turned to day. Running through the snow with the light came the armies of hell. Thousands of demons, maybe tens of thousands, surrounded a monstrous being who actually was the source of the light. Agzamoth was here in all his vile glory. He had fed upon thousands of people and it had grown him to such proportions that he dwarfed some of the buildings he passed. His stride was callous, destroying any of his minions unlucky enough to be caught underfoot. His gaze was filled with contempt, both for his followers and those arrayed against him. Fetid winds blew with his every exhale, filling the square with the stench of rot. His voice boomed out into the Fimbulwinter of his own creation, it's tone equal parts enticing melody and heartrending dread.

"Woe unto you, my children," sang it's angel's voice

"Come to me to receive thy just reward," snarled it's demon's howl

"And reward you I shall!" the voices combined in a chorus of doom.

"Well, I'm not your kid," Rang out a voice as chilling as that of the demon's, "but I will take you up on that reward."

The Insomniac stood from where he sat. He began to walk at the mass of demons, his every step cracking the snow covered pavement. A statue stood in his way and he simply walked through it as if it didn't exist. The twenty foot marble hero exploded with thunderous force. Before the dust could settle, the Insomniac became a blur. His bathrobe seemed to stretch as he covered the distance to the monsters in a blink of an eye. The demons who stood in his path didn't stand for long. Some flew nearly fifty feet in all directions when he slammed into the mob. I guess he figured out who woke him on his little own. I didn't know who to feel sorrier for…

When the Demonlord appeared, the fighting around the building slowed to a stunned halt. When the Insomniac went after the demons, the battle started back up as if someone hit a switch. To the south, skeletons and zombies pushed mindlessly against the barricades. To the west, Bloodmoon and Eagle battled as other heroes tried to fend off the wolfpack. To the north, hundreds of demons clawed at and died from the Insomniac. His every blow killing dozens, their sheer numbers holding him back from their lord.

But their lord didn't want him held back. Agzamoth had watched this one from the moment he spoke. Any being in this realm who had the courage to speak to him in that manner was a being either mad with bravado or worth watching. After the loud one attacked his minions, Agzamoth knew he was worth watching. And watched he had, with each strike from the Insomniac the demonlord learned how to defeat him. With each demon killed, Agzamoth began to see a weakness.

Three giant strides carried the monstrous Agzamoth into reach of the mad human. Swiping downward, he was sure he would spear this flesh sack and savor his death. The Insomniac had different plans. Diving towards the ground, the Insomniac cut through the pavement like it was water. Agzamoth looked around in puzzlement for a second before the Insomniac burst through the ground behind him. The demon lord began to turn as the Insomniac slammed into him from the side.

Agzamoth was surprised. The human had appeared to be a strong adversary but he had not expected just how strong. The little human landed punch after punch on the side of his head before the demon could finally grab him. Holding the struggling human away from his body, Agzamoth threw him as far as he could. The Insomniac was still on the way up when he disappeared from sight. He would more than likely survive the trip even if he achieved escape velocity and ended up in space. Agzamoth watched the human cut through the night air and then turned his vile gaze back towards us. The demons began to move towards City Hall from his unspoken command. And then Jinx and Junkyard arrived.

Both teams swooped down from the east and immediately began to fight off the zombies to the south and the wolves to the west. Their numbers pushed back the tide. Within moments, Bloodmoon had been taken down by Gun Control. He fired a blue capsule at the werewolf and when it hit it covered the werewolf in a cloud of silver blue particles. The particles absorbed the moonlight and weakened the werewolf. In his weakened state, Bloodmoon was quickly knocked out from one of Eagle's powerful punches. With the werewolf unconscious, the wolves that followed him transformed back into shivering, naked humans.

The army of the dead was not so easy rebuffed. The reinforcements held them back but that was about it. The sheer numbers of undead who had no fear and felt no pain were advantage enough versus the added firepower. The civilian militia fired salvo after salvo of energy blasts into the mob to little effect. Graveyard would not be so easily defeated.

By the time that Bloodmoon had fallen and the armies of Graveyard had been stalled, the mass of demons smashed into the northern defenses. Heroes from the western barricades rushed alongside Stiletto's team to push back the onslaught. With all the reserves thrown into the mix, the demon horde's charge was blunted and the defenses held.

Behind me, the door to the roof opened and a dozen women came running onto the roof. They all carried long range laser cannons. The women rushed to the edge of the building and crouched down behind the short wall. Propping the weapons on the wall for stability, the women began sniping with amazing accuracy. Demons and undead fell with nearly every shot. For a moment, it looked like we were doing well. But only for a moment.

Agzamoth grew tired of watching and decided he wanted to play. His great wings unfurled and bloated out the night sky. They beat once, then twice, then he was flying over the battlefield. He swooped down and landed within the barricades with an earthshaking crash. Heroes, demons, and civilians went flying. The demon lord lashed out with eight foot long claws and everyone in his path died. I couldn't wait any longer.

My muscles tensed as I prepared to leap out into space. For a moment, time stopped. The world seemed to freeze in it's tracks as Agzamoth's head slowly turned to face me. Strange music played in my ears and visions clouded my eyes. Then a ghostly figure stepped between the two of us. My sight cleared as Shimmer pointed and said something. He repeated himself after a second and I realized he wanted me to look over my shoulder. I turned.

Hundreds of heroes were appearing through the snowstorm. Black helicopters with scary looking missiles flew alongside them. My call for help had gotten through, the nation's heroes were here with the military backing them up. The copters dove down onto the army of undead and began unleashing hell on them. It seemed fitting to me.

The heroes went after the demon lord and the power unleashed was something never seen on this world. Lighting crackled, fire raged, ice formed, thunder rippled, and energy sizzled as Agzamoth howled in agony. The fabric of reality itself seemed poised to break when suddenly the demon lord shrugged mightily and threw off the attacking heroes.

Time froze again as the demon lord turned to face me. His eyes burned a challenge and my blood sang in response. The Lance I carried began to quiver in anticipation. My fingers ached to grab it, my heart longed for its power. I watched myself pull out the lance like I was watching someone else do it. It was time.

I looked at Shimmer with fear in my eyes but he simply nodded to me. I was right, now was the time to use the Lance. My leg muscles tensed and uncoiled as I leapt at Agzamoth's throat. His hands lashed out and swatted me to the ground. I slammed into the pavement with tremendous force but I felt none of it. The Lance protected me. The Lance controlled me now. And it felt right.

Standing, I pushed off again as the demonlord struck were I had been laying. Huge chunks of concrete flew into the air as his claws sliced into the pavement. Snow exploded upwards with the impact. I flipped in midair and landed on his knee. He seemed to move in slow motion as I leapt up and rammed the Lance into his heart. Black blood gushed out as I jerked the Lance loose from his chest. His howl froze the battle and even the undead seemed to try to turn away and run. Agzamoth began shaking and quivering uncontrollably. Cracks appeared in his skin and quickly chunks of rotted black and red flesh began to slide off of him. As he twitched and jerked, I fell to the ground painfully. The Lance no longer was protecting me, it had drank its fill for the moment.

I looked up in time to see the demonlord grimace down at me in rage. His forked tongue poked out of his mouth as he raised his fist over his head. Rotting flesh fell in chunks as his arm screamed down towards me. I held the Lance up reflexively and as the demon lord's blow met my upraised hand a blinding flash filled my vision. The flash was the last thing I remembered.

Epilogue

"This is the end."
—Jim Morrison

The kid turned off the tape recorder. He scribbled a few notes down on his notepad and looked back up at me. He had the fresh faced look of someone just out of college. The kid even had the pudgy vestiges of baby fat in his face and the red flush of a recent acne attack.

"What happened with Michelle? And the Lance?" asked the kid, "and what happened after you blacked out?"

"Some things I will keep to myself," I replied patiently, "I already explained that."

The kid nodded as if he understood. But he didn't understand. How could he understand that there was no story with Michelle. She and I were happy and peaceful. We enjoyed each other's company and loved spending quiet time together. There was no way I was going to risk spoiling that over some rinky-dink interview for Superheroes Quarterly.

And the kid didn't understand about the Lance. Hell, I didn't understand the Lance. I knew that it killed Agzamoth with ease and that when he died, his demon hordes died with him. I knew that Agzamoth's death left Graveyard as the sole bad guy and he was quickly captured. But that was about it. The whys and the hows involving the Lance were beyond me. Even if I was the one holding it.

The kid gathered his stuff up and made the usual small talk. He thanked me for my time and promised to send me a copy of the article.

He seemed excited about shaking my hand so I tried to appear as if meeting him had been important. But it hadn't been, at least not to me.

The important thing was visible as I watched the kid leave City Hall from my corner office. The people of this city were going about their business like nothing was different. They picked their way around the rubble as they ran errands and went to work. They stepped over the broken glass on their way to the movies or bowling. The city and its people were still alive and kicking. That's what was important.

As I mused over the view, I felt a presence behind me. I was about to address Shimmer when I realized that it wasn't him. Shimmer didn't breath. I turned slowly and made a show of being surprised at Mediator. He wasn't fooled.

"Please," he said, "don't act like I surprised you. I know I didn't"

"Being a mind reader helps," I shot back with a grin, "how long have you been here?"

"Long enough to hear you dodge the question about the Lance," he answered.

"Was it that obvious?" I asked.

"Painfully obvious," he replied.

"What is it?" I asked.

"It's my spear. I used to be a roman soldier," he replied, "I've come to reclaim it. No man can resist its siren's call for long. Except for me."

"Here," I said as I pushed the leather case over to him, "I don't want it. Why did you ever give it to me?"

"You answered your own question. You don't want it," he answered, "the Lance of Longinus can only be held by the one who doesn't want to wield it. Otherwise, it will quickly consume whoever touches it."

"The Lance of Longinus?" I stammered, "You mean you're…"

"Yes. I am." he replied, "I have been paying for my sin since the moment I committed it."

"I…" I said, "This is just really hard to swallow."

"It's true. I am who I say I am and this is what I say it is," he said firmly.

"I can believe it after seeing what it and you are capable of," I replied.

182

"Good. You did well this time. The guys upstairs are pleased. Relax and enjoy your life. Teach the heroes of this city how to be heroes. Live and love with your woman," He said as he stood. "but be ready. This story isn't over yet. We will have need of you again one day. And that day is swiftly approaching."

"I'll be here," I said gravely.

"I know you will," he replied as he disappeared.

I watched the space were he had stood for a moment than I turned back to the window. Outside, people hurried to work or school or the grocery store or home. Outside, pools of sunshine warmed the day. Outside, children played innocently.

Off to the side of the plaza stood a dark alley. In it shapes moved and shadows twisted. In the deep blackness, the jungle lived.

The Concrete Jungle.

Printed in the United States
55973LVS00005B/136-150